QUEENS OF DEATH

BLOOD REIGN: AN ANTHOLOGY OF DARK ROYALTY

BLUDGEONED GIRLS PRESS

CONTENTS

Dedication

From D.A. Latham:

I dedicate this book to my best friend, Kimyona Dietter. Without Kim's constant love, support, and unending sense of humor, I wouldn't have had the nerve to make the move to start getting published. She's one of the best people I know, and I wouldn't know what to do without her. I'd also like to dedicate this book to Robert Dunn. A random piece of his art he posted inspired me to write Finding Heaven many years ago. I wouldn't have discovered my love of writing without that inspiration.

From Angelique Jordonna:

To Amanda McCord, who's always supportive of me, no matter what I'm trying to do. Music, writing, and anything else I decide to dig into and focus on. She's always there supporting and cheering me on. Second, this is for all of the readers, reviewers, and supporters of the indie horror community. You guys kill it and we all appreciate you.

FOREWORD

By Ruthann Jagge & Natasha Sinclair

"Those who could not be trusted remain consistent." —
Michael R. Collins "No Shelter Here"

In the earliest writings, references are made to royalty, whether real or perceived, as someone who behaves and carries themselves in a manner superior to others. Someone with strength and power and who commands and demands grandiose respect. The coveted title of a queen in modernity takes on many meanings in the position of a romantic partner, the head of a house or organized business endeavor, or one born to the position and a life of obligation and servitude—the queen bee. Whether it's been a title granted by scaling the ranks or through succession, a word that always comes to the forefront with the queen is power.

The queen is the most powerful piece on the chessboard; she commands the army to make sacrifices, and when she moves, none in her sights can escape—be her or spend your life trying to escape her. In both reality and royalty, many consider the role as little more than a pawn herself. There is undeniably a polarity at play with the notion and role of the queen depending on her throne's location.

Queens of Death is an original anthology full of shadows and impending doom. Gifted writers will introduce the reader to all manner of queens who take their title seriously and use it to wreak havoc on all they encounter.

Angelique Jordonna and Donna Latham, the names behind the book, are up-and-coming queens within the independent horror writing community. Angelique is an award-nominated author working tirelessly to help shine a focus on diversity and acceptance within the dark genres. Donna is a talented author who elevates the work of others through her thoughtful reviews and steadfast support. We've published in books together, laughed with, and have great respect for the pair, who've recently joined forces in their publishing imprint, Bludgeoned Girls Press. Anyone who knows us knows how much we value and relate to fiercely female-led collaborations.

Each story in this finely crafted anthology offers a fresh vision of the title in a vibrant assortment of unexpected imaginings every reader of the macabre can delight in. An elegant house in the style of a notable queen eager to consume. Desperation, refuge, and ethereal royalty disguised as disease. There is unimaginable carnage for queens who are betrayed. There's impending doom in the process of becoming and maintaining popularity as a fading monarch. Queens of all sizes and shapes demand devotion at a significant cost to their subjects, and those with heavy crowns and sparkling hopes as they stand proudly on stage among their young peers may learn harsh lessons. These pages give a platform to exiled monstrous queens with sharp weapons who lurk in nature's bowels.

All these women are shaped by legend, imagination, and superstition. They rule without mercy, with death close by as a trusted advisor. However, some queens that readers will encounter skillfully disguise themselves to move casually among us with nefarious intentions—with deep pockets and purses full of vials of deadly potions and folded paper curses. They crash black-tie events, wearing a smile while barely wrapped in expensive silk garments, bearing gifts, and casting spells while seducing fresh prey. Perhaps that prey tonight is you....

Queens of Death pays homage to the boldest sovereigns of our nightmares, appointed or self-designated, in the past, present, and future.

These queens wallow in a legacy of darkness. Turn the page, kneel, and bow low to the Queens of Death.

1

— • —

LONG LIVE THE QUEEN

BY ERIC BUTLER

NIK REACHED OVER AND took his sister's hand. He glanced around, noting the dying sunlight through the thick branches of the trees, and swallowed. Gonna be dark soon. He ignored the thought and instead glanced over at Sophia and offered a forced smile. He hoped to hide the fear growing in his belly from the girl. Now was not the time to have to deal with a scared five-year-old.

"It's getting darker," she whispered, echoing his unspoken thoughts. "Momma said we shouldn't be in the woods after the sun goes down."

"And we wouldn't be if you hadn't chased after those deer," he said, his cheeks instantly hot with shame. Is this how a future ruler behaves? Blaming others? His thoughts echoing his mother's lessons every day since the coup. As the oldest, he was responsible for making sure they followed the rules. Today, he had broken the two most important ones. Never leave Elias behind and never be in the woods after dark. He cleared his throat and held up the basket he carried in the other hand. "But then we wouldn't have found these wonderful blackberries."

"They're momma's favorite," she said, as if he didn't know. "If we're lucky, she'll be well enough to make a pie."

"Hmm," he offered noncommittally, knowing their future held tanned backsides and being sent to bed hungry.

Something flashed in his peripheral, and he turned his attention to the left. He squinted, straining to see anything in the growing shadows.

He picked up his pace, but after a few steps, it became clear that Sophia couldn't keep up.

"Slow down, Nik," she whined, squirming to pull her hand free.

He tightened his grip and pulled her closer. She let out a startled yelp and stumbled forward, regaining her balance by leaning into him. He paused and turned just enough so he could scoop her up. She wrapped her arms around his neck.

"That a girl," he said, clenching his jaw. "Hold on tight, and I'll get us out of the here."

The shadows crept closer, and soon a blanket of darkness covered the woods. A screech pierced the silence, and Sophie buried her face in his shoulder. Nik wondered what creature made such a cry. Maybe an owl? But he knew that was wishful thinking. Whatever had just cried out was larger and angrier than an owl, and while the creature's cry seemed far away, he knew sound could be distorted out in the forest. He glanced back but found only darkness. He wanted to be relieved but couldn't shake the feeling something was out there. Watching them.

A loud crack of wood came from the darkness off to their left, and Sopia flinched. She mumbled something, but he couldn't make out the words. He kept his eyes forward and prayed they didn't discover what was out in the woods with them. He pulled Sophia tighter to his chest and tried to ignore the sound of rustling leaves and snapping branches.

The undergrowth grew thicker, and Nik swerved to the right to avoid having to slow down. The tip of his left foot caught a root protruding up, and he stumbled forward. His ankle gave out, and he began to fall. A sharp yelp came from his sister, and he twisted his body to cushion her from the hard packed earth rushing towards them. There was a sudden jab of pain when he slammed into the ground and the air whooshed from his lungs. His head snapped back, and stars filled his vision.

He struggled to stay conscious. Sophia rolled off his chest and reached out to press her fingertips against his cheek. "Nik?"

He offered a groan to let her know he was alive, but she continued to poke at him.

"I do not think that is helping, child," a woman said firmly, but Nik detected a note of amusement in the tone. "What are you doing out here so late in the day?"

Nik's eyes fluttered open and for a moment, he struggled to see through the shadowy haze. When his vision cleared, he found Sophia bathed in a soft light, holding up the basket. With a quiver in her voice, she said, "We picked berries for our mother, but Nik dropped them when we fell."

The light flared brighter and drove the darkness away. "We can't have that, now can we child?" the woman said as stepped closer to Sophia.

A smile bloomed on his sister's lips, and she began to scoop up the scattered berries. "Oh, thank you."

Nik shifted his gaze to the woman. She was tall, easily the same height his father had been, and though she wore a hooded cloak, he could see enough of her face to realize it was one he had seen before. But where? He blinked a few times and struggled to remember. The woman reached up with her free hand and pushed the hood back onto her shoulders. The image of a book flashed in his head, and his breath caught. She was more beautiful in the flesh than what he remembered drawn in that old book in his parents' library. The last queen to rule his homeland, Tyre. But how could that be possible?

The woman he read about fell out of favor with the gods, and then her subjects, who stripped her of her crown and sent her into exile to die. When he asked why, his parents had different answers. His father blamed her infidelity, whatever that meant, but his mother waited for them to be alone to tell Nik that the gods were jealous of her beauty, and they turned her subjects against her. She hugged him tight and reassured him that it was nothing more than a parable. And yet, seeing this woman before him, he could see why the gods were jealous. Except it's not the same woman ... it was a bedtime story.

She held up a lantern in her right hand, focusing the light on the ground around his sister. The woman squatted and held out her slender left arm to point to some berries missed off to the side of Sophia. The lantern swung further away from her, but the shadows only seemed to enhance her beauty. Her head turned slightly, and she studied him from the corner of her eye.

"A few more, and she'll have them all," she said to Nik before sliding her attention back to his sister.

Sophia leaned forward and scooped the final berries up, laughter bubbling past her lips when she dropped them back into the basket. The woman pressed her hand against his sister's face and held it there for a moment.

"Such a pretty little thing," the woman murmured. "So full of life."

Nik could tell that Sophia was enjoying the attention, and he was surprised at the sudden jab of jealousy he felt. He struggled to rise, managing to sit up before a wave of pain washed over him. He grew lightheaded and steadied himself by pressing his hands against the ground. While he knew he should be concerned by the pain, all he could think about was how desperate he was to feel her touch against his skin.

Heat flushed throughout his body, and colored his cheeks red, but this time not from anger or embarrassment, but from something he'd never felt before. Something he couldn't quite place his finger on. The woman's head swung towards him, and she stared at him with questioning eyes.

"And what of you, Nikolas? Do you normally leave all the work to your sister?"

His chest tightened when their eyes met, and while he thought he mumbled an answer, all he could hear was the pounding of his heart. Her eyes flashed, and though he knew it must be a trick of the light from her lantern, they began to glow. The woman stood, and Nik wished his mother was there. She would know what to do. He blinked away the sudden tears in his eyes, unsure if they were caused by the pain or a sudden realization that he might never see her again. Just like Father. She shined the light down on him and uttered a loud tsk.

"Goodness," she said, the concern in her voice absent from her eyes. She continued, speaking over her shoulder to Sophia, "I scolded your poor brother, and here he lies injured. Stay where you stand, little one, so I can take care of him."

Nik glanced down, his breath catching at the sight of the jagged end of a stick protruding through a tear in his blood-soaked shirt. There was another spike of pain, and his stomach rolled. The woman placed the lantern on the ground and squatted before him. She slid her finger under his chin and raised his head until their eyes locked once again.

So beautiful, he thought, unaware he said the words aloud.

With a wry grin, she wrapped her fingers around the wood and leaned close enough to brush her lips against his ears. "It came at a cost, but you can help me repay them for what they did." Nik blinked. How can I help? She wiggled the stick, and he gasped. Her breath tickled his skin, and with a husky voice, she continued. "Will you help me?"

The woman pulled back, and a chill ran through Nik's body. For a split second, he thought it might be a trick of the shadows, but the cold knot of fear tightening in his belly told him otherwise. Her pale face was longer, thinner than before. Her eyes now were shining, shifting from yellow to red to black and back again, and her plump, red lips moved silently with unheard speech. After what seemed like an eternity, she pulled them back to expose ever growing fangs. A thin, forked tongue slithered over her teeth and the tip quivered inches from his face.

He stared blankly ahead. A terrible scream ripped from his chest as she began to pull harder on the stick, his sticky wet blood oozing onto her hand. His vision went white from the pain, and he thought her lips pressed against his. The sensation disappeared in a split second, and he began to sway.

"NIK. SOPHIA," a man called out.

"HERE, Uncle Elias," Sophia said, her voice cracking with emotion. "Hurry, Nik's hurt."

The woman released the stick with a hiss, and Nik tumbled backward. He watched the woman lift her hand to her mouth and run her tongue over the bloody gore that covered her fingers. "Mmm, so tasty," she said, snatching her lantern from the ground.

The woman blew out the light, and Sophia issued a short scream of terror as the area plunged into darkness. Nik struggled to stay conscious, and whispered his sister's name over and over, hoping to lead her to him.

Light suddenly flared above him, and he realized his uncle was staring down at him.

"Thank the gods, Nik," Elias said, swinging a torch back and forth. "Now, where is your sister?"

Nik's head lulled about, and a fat tear slipped from the corner of his eye. "With a ghost," he murmured before passing out.

ELIAS CARRIED NIK THROUGH the woods. The boy was just big enough that he had to discard the torch, so he took slow and careful steps. He was pretty sure he was headed in the right direction, but prayed for a split in the trees so he could catch a glimpse of the stars above. He never was one to enjoy any time in the wilderness and simply felt lost when he couldn't see the sky. *What I wouldn't give to be far from this hell and close to the sea once again.* He looked down at his nephew and his chest tightened. That day would never come if anything happened to the boy.

Light up ahead pulled Elias from his thoughts, and he sped up, pulling Nik closer. The boy issued a low groan. *Foolish children,* but the thought held no malice towards them. No, the real anger he saved for himself. He was given one duty, and he allowed his melancholy to jeopardize everything. *Will Iris ever forgive me?* He frowned. *If anything happens to the boy, will I?*

There was still a chance that another heir resided in the Queen's belly, but they wouldn't know for sure until his sister gave birth. And yet, even then, they could not return home right away. There were still too many revolutionaries about, all of whom would have no issue slaughtering innocent children to get their way. So, until they could make their triumphant return, they were to hide in the shadow of the one place no sane man would ever think of going. These damnable woods.

His frown deepened. At first, Elias had rejected the rumors as superstitious nonsense, but after months of living so close, he knew better. There was something wicked about this place, and he felt a little more drained of hope with each day spent in its accursed shadow. At first, he worried it was affecting the others as well, but lately, it was all he could do to get dressed. And yet when Iris begged him to watch the children so she could rest, he did not make the connection. Fool.

Elias flinched at the memory of his nodding and promising to keep an eye on the children, all the while knowing he would do no such thing. He remembered thinking they were old enough to watch after themselves and then disappeared into the barn to drown his sorrows. When he awoke, the sun was setting, and the children were gone. More than a Fool. He cursed his weakness and prayed it was not too late to make amends.

The light ahead grew brighter, and he realized they were approaching a fire burning in the center of a small clearing. Over the flames hung an iron cauldron, which was filled with a thick black liquid that bubbled and churned. A clothesline ran from a colorful caravan parked off to the side to a tree across the way. A few chickens wandered about, and he wondered what kept them from running off.

He stepped into the clearing and called out, "Hello? Is anyone here?" He took a deep breath to try again, unsure if he hadn't been heard or was simply being ignored.

"Not so loud," a voice hissed. "Or you will draw her attention."

He spun around, unsure where the command had come from. All he found were the chickens, no longer pecking at the ground, but instead, studying him. One of the birds, the plumpest by far, stepped closer and tilted its head.

Did the bird …? The thought trailed off. I may be a fool, but am I not crazy? Am I?

The door at the center of the caravan swung open, and a withered old woman exited. She walked with a hitch and leaned against the cane in her right hand. While her dress was a dull grey in color, she was wrapped in colorful scarves so bright they made his eyes hurt. She pulled up a few feet away and offered a crooked smile.

"Were you about to talk to Bethanie?" she asked, the amusement plain in her soft tone, and pointed to the chicken standing between them.

He shook his head; worried words would betray him. Instead, he held Nik out and said, "We need help. My nephew is injured, and my niece is missing."

The smile slid from the woman's lips, and she hobbled closer. She reached out and gently probed with her fingers around the entry wound. "Were you not warned of the dangers of these woods?"

Nik flinched at the woman's touch, and Elias wondered if he should pull the boy away.

"Well?" the woman asked, her voice while still soft, now resonated with command. She glanced up, and they locked eyes.

"Yes," Elias replied in a whispered voice, shifting his gaze before continuing, "Children don't always listen."

"And yet, I sense this was not their fault. This wound should not be the death of the boy, but I cannot say what will become of your niece if she is indeed lost out here."

The crone turned and began to walk back to the caravan. After three steps, she glanced back and with her head, motioned to Elias to follow her. He lurched forward, desperate to save at least one of the children. They entered the caravan, and he laid Nik down on the bed attached to the far wall. The crone pointed to the doorway.

"Rest by the fire. If I need you, I will call."

Elias paused, his gaze moving from his nephew to the woman and back to the boy.

"The boy is special," he said, stepping over to the doorway. "Nothing can happen to him."

"Then you should have never brought him to this damnable place."

———◆O◆———

SOPHIA RAN. SHE WASN'T sure where she was going, just that she needed to be away from the pretty lady. But she's not pretty. She tried to forget
what she saw right before the light went out, but she knew it would
haunt her until the day she died. Gasping for breath, she tried to run
faster, but the pain in her side sapped her strength.

A gap in the branches overhead allowed moonlight to stream through
and illuminate a felled tree just off to the right. Sophia slid to a stop and
fell to her hands and knees. She scrambled into the hollowed-out log and
crawled until she found a jagged rent that allowed her to peek out. She
pressed her eye to the opening and waited, her breath coming in short
pants.

Tears streamed down Sophia's cheeks, and she desperately wanted to
call out for help. But she remembered one of her mother's rules. When
you are hiding, never make a sound. Otherwise, the not so pretty lady
might find her first, and that made her bowels turn to water. She squeezed
her anus tight, desperate not to have an accident.

"Why do you run, child?"

Sophia's breath caught at the sound of the woman's voice. Her eyes
shifted around franticly, but she could not see anyone through the opening. The woman stepped into view and stopped walking just on the
edge of the moonlight. Sophia began to tremble, and bit down on her
bottom lip to stop herself from crying out. She watched the woman
glance around the woods.

"You cannot hide from me, child," she said, her voice like honey. She
tilted her head back and began to sniff the air. "Not when your fear is so
palatable."

The woman's gaze fell onto the log, and she stepped into the moonlight. Sophia watched with unblinking eyes as the woman reached behind her neck and pulled free the knot that held her garment up. The
dress slipped down her body and pooled at her feet. A sudden urge to

call out and beg for forgiveness overwhelmed Sophia, and she bit down harder until blood filled her mouth.

"After all these years, I find this form so restricting," the woman said, stretching out her arms and arching her back.

Sophia's eyes widened. Everything about the woman seemed to elongate, and the beauty of her face slid away to reveal a horrific visage beneath. The woman's lips pulled back, and long, sharp fangs grew out. She stepped out of the dress and pressed her legs together, but Sophia was drawn to the woman's hands, where the fingers now grew longer, and razor-sharp claws ripped through her fingertips.

"Do they still whisssper my name, child?" the woman asked, running her forked tongue across her lips. Bright yellow eyes fell on the log and flashed with excitement. "Are you taught to fear Lamia, as the gods did all those years ago?"

The woman lurched forward; no longer standing on two legs, but instead slithered forward on a thick snake like body. Sophia's bowels released, and she squeezed her eyes closed. She screamed when the woman slammed into her hiding spot and clawed at the opening. Lamia's nails nicked her cheek, and she tried to squirm away from the opening. The log rose, and soft laughter filled her ears, followed by the sharp crack of wood.

For a moment, Sophia felt like she was floating. Much like the day Nik took her to the river to teach her to swim. But the sensation, like the memory, flitted away, and she plunged to the ground with a cry. She lay on her back, desperate to regain the breath driven from her body by the fall. Her eyes grew wide when Lamia leaned over her and smiled, her forked tongue quivering in anticipation.

"Don't worry, child. I promise to reunite you with your family soon enough."

———◦———

ELIAS WOKE WITH A yelp. Something was jabbing him in the chest, and after a moment, he realized it was the crone's cane. "Enough, I'm awake."

"I've stitched the boy up," she said, giving him one more poke before shuffling to the pot and grabbing a spoon to stir the liquid. It bubbled and belched, and she nodded her approval. "He will live, but I cannot say the same about your niece."

Elias sat up and rubbed the sleep from his eyes. "And why is that?"

"Lamia," the crone said as if the one word explained it all. She glanced at him and frowned. "This name brings you humor?"

Elias shook his head. "From a story told to scare children? A fable is why we were warned to avoid this place?"

"You were warned because death resides in these woods," the woman said with a shuddered breath. "And while it is a fable in its own way, it is no children's story."

He struggled to his feet, his joints stiff and achy from sleeping on the cold, hard ground. He didn't know exactly what she meant, "Nonsense. Lamia died centuries ago, exiled on an island far from home, not roaming the forest like a wild animal."

"The truth was too much for them to bear," the crone said, spitting off to the side. "For you see, the gods punished her first. They brought her children before her and made her watch them die. Each more horrible than the last, and at the end, when she was driven mad with grief, they took away two things - sleep and death. They wanted her to relive her punishment every second of the day. What they didn't plan for was her punishment quickly becoming their punishment, as she began to kill any and every child she came across. The people began to blame the gods and started to turn from them. So, they found a way to take her soul and imprison it to a spot, but there was a catch. A mortal had to watch over her soul and make sure it stayed contained."

"I have seen the sacred texts. There is no mention of this. Impossible."

The crone shook her head. "Not impossible, but they were bigger fools than the gods. Because without her soul, she has become something even the gods fear."

Elias pointed towards the tree line. "I don't believe any of this. I have to find my niece."

"Be quiet and listen."

Elias blew out an exasperated breath and threw up his hands. After a moment, he tilted his head toward the forest. "I don't hear anything."

"Precisely," the crone said with a sigh. "Usually Lamia is circling my camp, waiting for me to make a mistake. Tonight, we hear nothing because for the first time in four hundred years, she has something to feed upon."

Elias stared at the woman with wide eyes as he tried to make sense of what the woman was babbling about. His eyebrows rose up and bewilderment was quickly replaced with horror. "Sophia. You think she is ... eating my niece?"

The crone nodded. "Otherwise, she would be here temping you to betray me."

"And why has she not just come and taken her soul back, if she is so powerful?" he snapped, trying to ignore the image of his niece's cold, dead body floating in his head.

"As long as this liquid boils, and I draw breath, she can neither enter this clearing nor leave these woods," the crone replied with a sigh. "But anyone outside this clearing in the woods will die."

Elias threw his arms out and leaned towards the old woman. "How is that even possible?" he spat each word out at her.

Elias glanced between the cauldron and the old woman's face. The crone is mad. A chill ran up his back at the thought. Did she really help Nik? A gust of wind blew through the trees, and the fire flared up, its flames licking up the sides of the pot before they retreated back.

"For my Queen," Nik said, his words monotone.

Elias jumped, shocked to find his nephew suddenly by the fire. The boy reached up and grabbed the lip of the pot, a loud hiss announcing when his flesh met the hot iron. He pulled down, and the thick black goop spilled down onto his face and chest.

"Noooo," the crone screamed, her arm stretched out to stop the boy.

Nik howled in pain as his skin began to blister and peel, exposing the dark red meat beneath. A cackle sounded from the trees, and an icy cold ball of fear twisted in Elias' belly. A shape darted past him. Pain flashed across his stomach, and he glanced down in confusion. Blood gurgled out from four deep slashes in his belly. His throat burned from the bile rising as he watched his intestines slip free and uncoil on the blood-soaked ground beneath him.

Elias grabbed at the wounds, squishing his insides as he tried to stuff them back inside him. Pain washed over him, and he fell to his knees. Vomit sprayed past his lips, and he whimpered. The crone's screams drew his attention to the fire, and he struggled to comprehend what he was seeing.

The most beautiful woman in the world stood over the body of the old crone. In her bloody hand, she held a still beating heart. Off to the side, Nik lay in a heap. His skeleton showing where the black goop had melted off parts of his flesh. The woman turned towards Elias and smiled.

"Your nephew's sacrifice will not be in vain," she said before taking a bite from the heart. "They will whisper his name in awe after I'm finished."

Elias' brow crinkled in confusion. "Finished?"

The woman squatted down and ran a bloody finger down his cheek to his neck. "Oh yes, I shall make the heavens and earth tremble from my fury. I just wish there was more time to relish this moment," she said, raking her claws across his throat.

THE DOOR TO A small house by the edge of the forest opened slowly. Iris tossed and turned and issued soft, mumbled words of confusion, but did not wake from her slumber. Lamia stepped into the room and inhaled. Yes, this is the place. There was no mistaking the scent. She moved closer, her bare feet shuffling against the rough wood floor. She looked down at the woman and smiled. She had found the source. Lamia stretched out her hand and held it just over the sleeping woman's belly. Her stomach grumbled, and she wondered how there was any room left.

"It's been so long, maybe I'll never be full," she whispered, closing her eyes to let the transformation take place. She found when she ate, it was always more satisfying as herself.

2

— · —

Filthy Lace on Bloody Skin

By M Ennenbach

THE MOMENT THE DOOR was opened, the intense scent of putrefaction rolled into the hallway with a greasy pungency which immediately triggered the detective's gag reflexes. The older man, Harrison, managed to choke his down. His partner, Miller, was not so fortunate, and unleashed a torrent of coffee and half-digested danish onto the warped floorboards of the apartment complex hallway.

Life in the slums was unkind on the best of days, a lesson hard earned by Harrison, which Miller found to be more difficult daily.

"Told you that danish was not needed," Harrison said as he pulled a handkerchief from his pocket and placed it over his lower face.

"Are you really going to start this shit again? Here?" Miller said incredulously as he spat the last of the bile to the floor.

"I wasn't the one wheezing on the stairs yesterday," Harrison rebutted with a raised eyebrow.

"It was five flights! Five. Ten sets of steps. You weren't exactly breathing easy either," Miller said as he wiped his mouth on his tie.

"Your tie? By the Weaver man, use your handkerchief!" Harrison said, aghast.

"Didn't think we'd be walking into an open sewer," Miller muttered.

"Shows just how little you know about how things work down here in Raven's Hook, rookie," Harrison said, then gestured for Miller to enter the dark apartment.

"Detectives Miller and Harrison of Her Majesty's Royal Police, is there anyone in here? Hello?" Miller shouted into the shabby living room. He flipped on a flashlight and let the beam cut through the room and turned to Harrison. "Clear."

Harrison nodded and entered the room. "There is something here."

Miller nodded and crossed the small room.

Harrison had a bad feeling, too long in the Hook. It had a way of seeping into your pores and filling you with a bone deep tired. The Hook took your expectations and found a way to make them worse. Every single day.

"Oh shit, Harrison, I found the source of the stench," Miller said.

Harrison shook his head and walked over to the open doorway where Miller stood. It was a bedroom, so much as there were a few boxes of clothes and mattress laying on the filthy linoleum floor. The corpse laying in the center of the room was definitely the source of the odor. She, it had been a woman once, lay in a painful rictus among a rust-colored stain which seemed to have soaked all the way through.

The corpse wasn't what made the bottom of Harrison's stomach drop, though. It was the black lines which crisscrossed the paper-thin flesh of the woman. Exactly like lace.

"Did you touch anything?" Harrison asked calmly over the thunder of his heartbeat in his ears.

Miller cocked his head. "I didn't think I needed to check for a pulse. What the fuck is that? Drug overdose?"

Harrison shook his head. "What's that in that box over there?"

Miller turned toward the boxes and had just begun to form the beginning of a question when Harrison pressed the barrel of his revolver to the back of his head. Before he could recognize what was happening, a small roar filled the silent room as a spray of brain slurry splatted onto the clothes.

"I'm sorry, Miller," Harrison said.

Harrison left the small apartment and closed the door behind him. He made his way down the stairway, carefully placing plastic zip ties around the doorknobs and anything he could find to keep the doors securely closed. He used his actual metal cuffs on the front doors to the building, then pulled out his radio.

"Harrison to base," he said.

"Base here, Harrison."

"Detective Miller is dead. I need a Firebug at my location immediately."

"A Firebug? What is the situation, Harrison?"

Harrison pulled a cigarette out of his pocket and lit it. He closed his eyes as the smoke burned in his lungs.

"Repeat. Harrison, what is the situation?"

"Bloody Lace. I've secured the doorways. But, if there is one corpse…"

"You're positive it's Bloody Lace?"

"Pretty goddamned sure, yes. I shot Miller after he discovered the corpse."

"Understood. Her Majesty thanks you for your service, Detective Harrison."

Harrison chuckled at that and took a long drag as sirens sounded in the distance.

"Her Majesty can go fuck Herself," Harrison said.

The loud discharge of the weapon and his lifeless body falling forward filled the foyer of the doomed building. Screams sounded from the upper floors as the residents realized they were trapped.

It didn't matter. Less than a minute later, the entire building was engulfed in flame. No one noticed another burning building in the Hook.

THE COURT WAS ABUZZ with gossip as they awaited the Queen to grace them with her presence.

"I heard half the Hook is ablaze!"

"The Bloody Lace is rampant."

"I heard a cobbler in Midtown had it."

The murmurs quieted as soon as the first of Her Majesty's entourage stepped into the throne room. Each of them chosen for their exquisite beauty, they strode into the room like art personified. There was no uniformity to the entourage of beautiful courtesans, except for perfection.

They were nothing compared to Her Majesty herself.

If the entourage were perfection, Lady Gertrude Beatrix the Thirteenth, embodied divinity itself. The sunlight itself seemed to pale as she stepped across the room. Her deep brown eyes drew the air from the lungs of the fortunate few to briefly meet her gaze. Her flawless alabaster skin reflected the sunlight streaming into the room in a rapturous nimbus. As was custom, a large contingent of the gathered nobility fainted as she passed, and also as custom, she took no notice.

Which was the heart of the problem concerning the stunning queen. She tended to pay no attention to anything which she did not find aesthetically pleasing.

It did not help that everything struck her as particularly ugly.

Yet nothing upset her delicate sense of taste quite as much as Ferdinand's, her personal servant, unfortunately small upper lip. He had tried everything. He grew a thick mustache. She found it to be too wooly and only managed to accentuate the smallness. He went to the apiary and paid a day's wage to convince the poor beekeeper to sacrifice two of her beloved bees to sting his lip. Her Majesty was quite upset when he missed the next week in the hospital due to anaphylactic shock.

Ferdinand had taken to wearing a silk handkerchief around his mouth in Her Royal presence. It did nothing to erase the memory of the tiniest of upper lips.

Ferdinand fretted over Her Majesty's dress, smoothing out the creases of her pearlescent dress, maximizing the sunlight playing pastel glimmers to accentuate Her divine perfection.

"I am sure they are as fine as you can hope to get them, Ferdinand. It is time for the petitioners. They most surely do not need to watch your tiny lip bead with sweat as you flail about," the queen stated flatly.

Ferdinand dipped his forehead to touch the floor, then scampered off to his perch just behind the throne.

Her Majesty nodded at the captain of Her Royal Guards, Eric Captain, a humorless man with an obsession for pockets. Eric bowed, the assorted baubles in his many pockets rattled loudly, causing his face to flush a deep crimson. He faced the crowd. "Her Majesty shall now listen to petitioners! But understand, Her Majesty does not suffer fools! All who wish to petition form an orderly line."

A nervous-looking man stood and approached Eric, who nodded and led him to a spot in front of the Queen. He bowed deeply at the waist and heads of sweat formed upon his brow as the Queen simply stared at him.

"Speak, man!" Eric rumbled.

"Yes. Yes. Your Majesty, The Hook has been burning for a week now. Three of my buildings have been consumed by flame. I beg you, please, I will be destroyed if all my properties burn to the ground," the man whined.

Her Majesty cocked her head at him, ever so slightly. "The Hook has been in need of cleansing for decades. I am sure the fire brigade has the situation under control."

Eric nodded, "Of course, your Majesty. I shall contact the Brigade Chief, but I am sure it is a controlled fire."

The man stared at Eric, mouth agape, "Surely you know the fires have been spread to control the outbreak?"

Her Majesty yawned, loudly, "What outbreak is it this year? Last year was the Sallow Fever, or was that two years ago? The plagues all run together after so long."

"Tis the Bloody Lace, your Majesty," Ferdinand muttered from behind the throne.

"Bloody Lace? How ridiculous," she replied.

"It is quite deadly, your Highness," the man muttered, perplexed at her response.

Eric stepped forward and grabbed the man by the shoulder, guiding him toward the exit. "Her Majesty will contemplate your concerns."

"Every night, the firebugs set more buildings on fire! The entire Hook shall be consumed!" the man pleaded, desperation heavy in his voice. "I will be ruined!"

"If you continue your outburst, you won't have to worry about the flames," Eric growled.

But the man's yelling stirred up the gathered petitioners, most of whom had come seeking some solution to the inferno brewing in The Hook. Voices began shouting, demanding action be taken to control the plague by means other than cleansing flame. This was most unusual when the Queen held court. She seemed bewildered by the building anger. Yet as it continued, her eyes grew colder and her jaw set.

"Ferdinand," she hissed.

"Yes, Your Highness?" Ferdinand asked with a shaking voice, of all the people sitting in court, he alone knew by her tone just how angry she was becoming.

"What is this Bloody Lace?" she asked low enough for only his ears.

"A fever, followed by lines of open sores which look similar to lace. Quite contagious, simply being near someone who has developed the wounds is almost certain death. Upon the first signs, a firebug is called out to eradicate the source," he explained softly.

Her Majesty sat up a bit on her throne, the petitioners still drowning on, but lost momentarily. "That sound delightful. Minus the fever and fire," she pontificated. "Someone find me pictures of this Bloody Lace," she announced to the room.

The room went silent, except for the jangling of pockets, as Eric escorted the petitioner to the doorway. His murmurs to the guard at the door carried before the large doors opened and then slammed shut. The jangling of his return was hushed by the whispers of the crowd.

Eric stood, red faced, and composed himself. "Who is next? And no more questions about the Book until Her Majesty has all the facts!"

No one stood. Worried faces and wringing hands were all the answers needed.

"Then this has been quite enough for the day. Be gone," the queen said with a dismissive wave.

The crowd began grumbling and Eric slammed his heels together. Each guard took a step forward with a hand on the bolt of their weapon. "The session has been adjourned. Proceed in an orderly fashion from the hall. Now!" Eric shouted.

Soon, the hall was empty except for Her Majesty, Ferdinand, and Eric. The tapping of her nails against the ivory armrest of the throne echoed in the chamber. Captain Eric Captain tried and failed to hide the slight wince as each nail clicked loudly. The fingers of his right hand were pale from where they clutched one of his many pockets.

Her Majesty noticed, she noticed everything. Her vacuous nonchalance was a byproduct of not caring enough to hide her obvious disinterest in everything. She had drawn when she was a happy young girl. But her mother found it distasteful. The princess was too beautiful to be hidden behind an easel. If she insisted on the arts, she would dance. Young Gertrude had despised dance from the first time she laced up her slippers. Her mother insisted and had her drawing supplies burnt.

She learned by watching her mother. The center of attention does not needto be a beautiful blossom, rather a spider disguised as a beautiful blossom sitting in the center of a web she had woven.

A loud rapping came from the doors, and Eric nodded to the guardsmen to open them. He strode across the hall, pockets jangling and retrieved a folder from the red-faced soldier, knocked his heels together and walked back to the throne, where he bowed deep at the waist (hoping no one noticed how flushed it made his face) and presented the folder to her.

Ferdinand rushed around the throne and opened the folder which lay on Her Royal lap, "I must warn you, milady, this is a horrid disease. The sight may be too much for Her gentle disposition."

The Queen glared at him. "If I must see that lip of yours on a daily basis, I am sure I can stomach a few pictures of a disease."

Ferdinand flushed nearly as red as Eric had when he bowed and nodded, "Of course, Your Majesty. My apologies."

She gasped at the first image. A younger woman laid nude upon a bloodstained bed. The lace ran across the entirety of her body, blossoming in angry red swirls where the flesh had crystallized. Ferdinand leafed through the images, and Her Majesty leaned forward, eyes wide.

She looked at Eric with tears in her eyes. "It is beautiful."

Eric sputtered for a moment, unsure how to respond, "This plague is deadly, sweeping through the Hook faster than the fires can purge."

She stared at Eric, unblinking.

Eric nodded, flustered. "But yes, Your Highness, it is quite the sight to behold."

She smiled and nodded and handed Ferdinand to continue, "They have gone from the lowest to works of art through this glorious disease. I never expected it would take on such a magnificent form. These otherwise repugnant creatures have become the epitome of beauty."

Eric appeared conflicted. "Yes, Your Majesty, but allow me to add, the disease is not only fatal and highly contagious, but sheer torment for the poor souls afflicted."

She waved a hand dismissively. "I am sure it is horrendous, yes. A true shame. Have the Plague Maestro retrieve a few of the poor souls. Perhaps he can find a solution."

Ferdinand smiled, "The Maestro will find a cure, a wonderful plan, Your Majesty."

She nodded, noncommittally, and stared at the pictures, tracing her fingers along the delicate patterns.

A WEEK PASSED, AND still the fires raged in The Hook. The crowded hall murmured, a buzzing hornets' nest of unhappy nobles, as they awaited The Queen's arrival. The large doors opened and the entourage of beauty swept into the room, but today the low murmur continued. Captain Eric looked about the room with a wary eye, one hand on the hilt of his sword, yearning to grab the sidearm on his hip. He nodded once to the guards at the doors, and Ferdinand, wearing a silken mask across his lower face, stood in the doorway and bowed deeply at the waist as Her Majesty walked past him. The crowd went silent, but again, the persistent buzz continued after she passed.

After Ferdinand finished straightening her dress, Gertrude murmured just loud enough for him to hear, "The silken mask only serves to remind me of your atrocious lip."

Ferdinand didn't say anything, just nodded before he scurried around the throne to assume his customary spot, causing Her Majesty to nod petulantly at the captain of Her Royal Guards, Eric Captain, a humorless man with an obsession for pockets. Eric bowed, the assorted baubles in his many pockets rattled loudly, causing his face to flush a deep crimson. He faced the crowd. "Her Majesty shall now listen to petitioners! But understand, Her Majesty does not suffer fools! All who wish to petition form an orderly line."

Even the Queen seemed to sense the tension in the room. Of course she did, but the fact it was noticeable, was not missed by the nobles. It caused them to look about nervously and the murmuring increased in pitch until Eric nodded at the guards around the room who all slammed the butts of their spears onto the marble floors which subdued the crowd nearly instantly.

Momentarily, at least.

A short man with a luxurious beard and prodigious belly nervously stood and bowed as low as he could. He looked at Eric, who eyed him suspiciously before nodding curtly. The man cleared his throat and his hand nervously clutched at his long beard, "Your Majesty, my husband and I have shoppes in The Rookery, yet our business has dried up over the last few weeks."

The Queen's lips pursed as she glared at the man. "And your suffering business is the crown's problem in what way?"

The man cleared his throat again and seemed on the verge of pulling a tuft of beard hair out, "The Bloody Lace, Your Majesty. The nobility will not venture into The Rookery any longer. The smoke from The Hook has grown, so thick in The Rookery, there is a persistent haze."

The murmur grew in intensity. Once again, the spears slammed down, and silence reigned. But now every eye was on the Queen, and the tension crackled in the air.

Instead, it was Ferdinand who stepped forward and removed his mask and kissed the man on the mouth as the entire assembly gasped.

"Ferdinand! Explain yourself right now!" the Queen roared.

The room was completely silent, as if all the air had been sucked from it as Ferdinand slowly turned around and looked at The Queen. Before he could utter a word, though, Eric stepped forward and, in a smooth motion,motion drew his sword and sliced Ferdinand's head clean from his shoulders.

His headless body stood in defiance for a frozen moment before a geyser of crimson erupted into the air, along with Eric's call, "Seal the Hall!"

The doors slammed shut as the crowd burst out into panicked shouting. The guards slammed their spears down repeatedly until the dull boom and Eric's calls for silence reduced the bare panic into a barely contained roaring gale.

The Queen stared at Ferdinand's head glaring up at her from the floor. Most importantly, at that offensive fucking lip of his. Except now it was glorious. The first lines of Bloody Lace in angry red called to her eyes. And then she frowned and stood up and approached the head and lifted it by the hair.

"Your Majesty! He has The Bloody Lace! Drop that immediately!" Eric shouted.

The Queen looked at him with a shocked expression, "It isn't The Bloody Lace. It is a tattoo. The idiot got it tattooed on his face for me."

This was lost as the crowd surged towards the now barred doors after hearing The Bloody Lace shouted. All except The Queen and the strangely gnomish looking man who had taken the brunt of the blood fountain's eventual giving in to gravity.

The Queen shrugged and dropped Ferdinand's head to floor and returned to her throne and sat down. She glared at Ferdinand once more as she tried to straighten her own dress and noticed a slight drip of blood had gotten onto the hem.

It was impossible to tell how many people were killed in the initial surge to the door. But it became easier to tell who died after by the spear wounds in the heavily ventilated corpses. When it was clear, the crowd would not be calmed with mere threats, the sharp heads fo the blades sliced open the stomachs of the nearest unfortunate souls.

The various liquids which happily sloshed from the now emptied stomach cavities made the marble floors slick as the panic of not just a deadly contagious disease, but of three-foot of hammered steel, made the closest people push and slip. This made the stabbing easier as they scrambled about in the viscera for purchase to regain their footing. Which was made more difficult as the spear heads punctured kidney and spine alike.

One man caught the razored tip just above his anus, which was eradicated a fraction of a second later before the rest of the blade drove into his lungs before being pulled back out, along with most of his ravaged intestines.

Eric stood at the edge of the crowd, demanding they cease, while at the same time his sword cut through flesh and bone in half moon arcs which flung blood in arcs, inciting further chaos as the crowd slammed against their broken compatriots at the doors. Someone slammed into his side, and he felt hands all over him as he fought back. One wrenched his pistol from his hand. He fought valiantly until the sheer numbers overwhelmed him.

The Queen watched dispassionately as Eric went down. Her eyes widened as the noble stumbled out of the pack and pressed the gun to a guard's head and unleashed a spray of skull fragments into the face of the poor bastard standing next him. Then she watched as the gun shakily turned and trained on her. She cocked her head and watched a spear head erupt through the woman's throat. The woman wobbled and fired three shots, two hit one of her perfect courtesans in her shapely leg. The Queen made a mental note to have a nice basket sent with her release papers.

The Queen sighed and stood. Her courtesans stared at her, and she bade them to stay. Then she walked through a secret door behind the throne, which slid shut with a resounding slam behind her.

"Your Majesty, are you injured?" a guard said as she stood before him.

"I am fine. Have the Hall gassed and thoroughly cleansed," she replied with a wave. "Have my ladies ready. I must be bathed and changed immediately."

"Yes, Your Majesty. At once," the guard said, waving at his second, who took off in a sprint.

"What is your name, soldier?" The Queen demanded.

"Brad, Your Highness, Brad Tierney," he said at once.

"Not anymore. It's now Brad Captain, Captain of my royal guard," she replied.

"Yes, ma'am!" he answered with a deep bow.

She nodded. "Send for the Plague Maestro as well. Enough of The Hook has burned. He needs to release the cure, and he needs to bring details on what he creating next."

Captain Brad went pale and nodded. "Yes, Your Majesty."

But she had already begun walking away.

3

—·—

A Queen's Undying Love

By Chisto Healy

VALENTINE STARED AT HER own image on the TV screen. She watched with tears in her eyes as the character she was better known as said, "Hey there. It is I, Valentina, the queen of your darkest desires."

She cringed at the sound of herself doing that ridiculous Dracula voice. She was from Tennessee. But it was what people wanted. Why did it matter? She wondered. They were all just jerking off, anyway. She watched a montage of herself with dicks, real and plastic alike, moving in and out of every hole she had in every position the director could conceive of. No one ever seemed to be turned off by the sad, empty look in her eyes.

The money wasn't bad, she told herself, at least now that she had become somewhat of a celebrity, but it was a hollow life, as hollow as she was. The ad ended with Valentina wiping blood off of her lips and telling the viewer the price of her new film.

"I'm a goddamned movie star," she said with a sniffle.

"Right on both accounts," a voice said from behind her.

Valentina sighed and turned around. "I said I wanted privacy. Please, just leave me alone."

"Oh shit, you're not going to drink me," the young man before her said, adjusting his glasses.

"I'm not thirsty," she said. "Please leave."

"Um... Leo wants you on set."

"I told him I was done for today. I'm sore, I'm tired, and I'm honestly just over it."

"I uh...told him that, and he said, 'Go get her!' and yeah...so, here I am."

Valentine lowered her gaze. She had chosen this when she first died. She didn't feel like anything mattered. She lost her family and friends. She lost her ability to conceive a child. She lost her ability to age with a partner. She lost everything. Being a fetish for people at least allowed her to be of some value to the world. At least, that's what she told herself. It was really just a way for her to meet her depression head-on, to accept what she thought she deserved. It got a little better when she won awards and went to events where she met her adoring fans. She signed autographs and took pictures with people, but at the end of the day, she knew they just wanted to fuck her and discard her, like the man who made her who she now was.

"So...you coming?" the young man asked her.

"What's your name?"

"Henry, ma'am."

"Yes Henry, I'm coming. Lead the way."

Valentina followed Henry out to the set where the director Leo was waiting, clipboard in hand. "We need to finish this. We have a deadline. Some new scenes have been written. I have some people. They're going to be an angry mob that aims to kill the vampire with pitchforks and torches and the works. You're gonna fuck them."

"I'm tired, Leo. I'm sore. Can't we do it tomorrow?"

"I'm afraid not, babe. Alan's only here for today."

"Alan?"

A huge beefcake of a man naked as the day he was born stepped out from behind a crudely painted cardboard castle wall. His manhood draped down by his left thigh like a drunken snake. He had dimples around the smile that said he was really proud of himself. Valentina sighed. "There are many more Alans," she said. "You can get another one tomorrow."

"Maybe, but not all of them." She looked where he was pointing. There were a bunch of naked people slipping on filthy medieval robes. "I got money in this, vampy. Just gimme my queen for a few more hours and you can take tomorrow off."

Valentina sighed. She closed her eyes and imagined shoving a stake into her own heart. When her eyes opened, she said, "Where do you want me?"

"That's my girl," Leo said. "Go stand in the archway, hand on each side, and let's see the boobs and the fangs."

"Fine," she said, opening her mouth to let him see her canines elongating. "But when this shoot is over, I'm done. I want more than this. I can't do this anymore."

"That would be great if you weren't under contract. Your vampy vag belongs to me until you've met the terms. Archway please."

Valentina stared daggers at him. Behind her eyes, she imagined sinking those fangs into his jugular and bleeding him dry, but the truth was that it wasn't him that made her into a thing to be used. She couldn't even blame the stranger who turned her that lustful Halloween night. She gave herself to him because she didn't care what he did to her. Even then, she was already gone. Valentina knew that she was the one to blame. She saw herself as nothing and she gave that idea to the world. But it wasn't too late, she told herself. Sure, she had lived a terrible self-deprecating life, but the truth was, it was only the beginning. She was middle-aged as far as mortals were concerned, but she wasn't mortal, not anymore. She opened her robe, exposed her breasts, and went to stand in the archway.

HOURS LATER, WHEN THE shoot was complete, Valentina limped her way towards the exit. She was hunched over, a hand on her lower back. It felt like her insides had been put in a blender. Her downstairs was on fire.

She winced when Leo patted her on the shoulder. "Great job today," he said. "People are gonna love it. We're gonna sell millions."

"Good. Then you won't need me anymore," she groaned.

"You want out, Valentina, you need to buy out. Can you do that?"

"Maybe when we sell those millions," she said, leaning against the wall to give her tired strained muscles a break. Her legs quaked beneath her.

Leo frowned. "Go get some rest."

Valentina nodded and went to the door. Carmine, who worked the desk, said to her, "What changed in you?"

"I'm sorry?" she asked, turning to look at him, one hand still on the door.

"Something is different about you lately. I mean, you've always seemed sad, but you seem sadder, lost."

"I'm over it, Carmine. I want out."

"Why? What changed?"

"Why does it matter to you?"

"Some of us actually care about you, Val. I just want to make sure you're going to be alright."

"I can barely walk. I feel like my insides have been scrambled. Everything burns and hurts. I've reached the point where sex actually disgusts me, makes me nauseous. Is that your version of alright?"

Carmine exhaled and looked down at his desk. When he looked back up, he said, "No, of course not, but it's been that way for a long time. This is not new. You have left here like that hundreds of times, maybe even thousands."

"What's your point?"

"What else is going on, Val?"

Valentina thought about the child. He lived in the back alley. He was filthy and smelled as bad as he looked, yet he always smiled. She hadn't met his parents and wasn't really sure he had any, but she knew he was part of a community. She'd seen them out there, warming themselves over barrel fires and drinking away their sorrows. Sometimes one would be found dead, and she found herself feeling envious that their pain had an end.

This boy, Thomas, he said his name was, had looked up at her, covered in grime as he was, and said, "You are always so sad. Why not just do something that makes you happy?"

As if it was so easy. She scoffed at him that day. The naivety of a child. He frowned at her reaction and said, "I just think if I could, I would change my life."

Valentina suddenly felt bad. She sat down on the stone wall across from the set and beckoned the boy to sit beside her. When he did, she said, "I'm sorry. How did you end up out here?"

The boy shrugged. "I don't really remember. I think I was a baby when the others found me. They've been good to me, but they don't have much. I sure would like a shower and some of those good chocolates, the ones rich people have...truffles."

Valentina couldn't help but laugh. "I can help you get both of those things. Would you like that?"

"Sure would," the filthy boy said with a smile, "but let's make a deal."

"A deal?"

The boy nodded enthusiastically and showed her his shining smile that glowed through the grime that painted his face. "You help yourself first and then you can help me. I'll be waiting."

Valentina sighed. "Helping you is easier."

"That's the point," the boy said. "Do the hard thing. Remember... you live forever, but I don't. Don't keep me waiting for too long."

Valentina laughed again. "What would I even do?"

"Whatever you want. Be nice to yourself. Go eat some truffles in the bathtub. Get married."

"That's the thing," she said, her face hanging like the ground beneath them was a magnet pulling at it. "I've always wanted that, but I can't have children. When I became a vamp, it took that away."

"I'm sorry/ I've always wanted a mom and dad. How about thinking about the things you can have instead of the things you can't? That's what the others always tell me."

Valentina fought tears and nodded. "You're right. Just because I can't have a baby doesn't mean I don't deserve love. Thanks for talking to me today, sweet boy."

Now, Valentina looked at Carmine and she said, "Nothing. I just met someone, and I want to be normal now. It's time."

She didn't wait for a response. Valentina opened the door and limped her way to the car. She didn't see the boy outside and hoped that he was alright.

As the days went on, Valentina's dream was hindered by sickness. It didn't make sense to her. Vamps weren't supposed to get sick. The only sickness she knew of that affected vamps was blood sickness. If you didn't feed or you fed too much, you got sick, violently if it had been long enough. It felt like your insides were trying to escape. She heard there was a vamp in Texas with leukemia, but she didn't know if it was true or not.

Whatever she was going through now... was something different. It was like before, like having the flu, but times ten. Every time she started to feel better, she got sick again. She had a fever, body aches, limbs like lead weights. She vomited more than she ate. "Fuck," she cried. "What the hell is happening to me?"

Valentina visited the doctor. He knew her condition. At this point, everyone knew her condition. She was famous or infamous more like. Either way, everyone knew who she was even if they didn't all admit it, because they didn't approve of her job choice. She didn't have to see the doctor much, though she did have a regular dentist. Today, Dr. Marlow took blood tests, mainly because he wasn't sure what else to do. When he came back, he was frowning.

"What is it?" she asked.

He took a deep breath and rubbed a hand over his bald head. "It seems you've contracted AIDS," he said. "It compromises your immune system and makes you very sick."

"Do I even have an immune system anymore? I'm dead."

"I know. I don't really um... understand how this works for your kind, but it seems to be very aggressive. We have treatments these days that have helped a lot of people have a normal life, but I... I don't know if they would work for you."

Valentina shook her head. "No. No, this isn't possible. Every person on set is supposed to be tested. If they test positive, they're not allowed on set. I don't have sex recreationally."

Dr. Marlow cleared his throat. "Is it possible that you...ahem... got it from something you... ate?"

Valentina groaned and rolled her eyes. "Christ, no. I feed during filming because it's part of what people want to see. Then I don't have to feed on anyone else. It's supposed to be a way to keep things safe. This shouldn't have happened."

"I'm very sorry. I'll go over the treatment options with you and see if anything appeals to you. You're immortal so it shouldn't be fatal, at least... I don't think, but I'm no expert on these things."

Valentina was thinking about the change she meant to make. She wanted to meet someone, to fall in love, to turn them and live forever together. She was going to leave the film industry and find a less self-destructive job. Well, that part was set in stone. Leo wouldn't let her back on set once he found out. But she couldn't turn someone, or she would give them the disease and cause them suffering. She felt like walking outside into the morning sun and incinerating herself.

"Valentina?" the doctor asked.

"Yes. Sorry," she said. "I-I need to find someone like me this has happened to, someone who can tell me what I'm in for..."

Dr. Marlow nodded. "I'll ask around and see if any of my colleagues can point me to someone, and I'll let you know what I find. If it's anything like normal human Aids, then it's going to be okay. Many people live a normal life with HIV now."

"What you've seen in my bloodwork? Is it like normal human HIV?"

The doctor sighed and averted his eyes. "No. It seems to have surpassed the HIV stages and gone straight to full-blown AIDS. I haven't seen anything so aggressive since the eighties, when we didn't know anything about it yet."

"Okay," she said quietly, her voice trailing off. She hopped down off the table, shivering and hugging herself. The room spun, and she swayed. That's when the nausea hit. "Let me know what you find," she said on her way out.

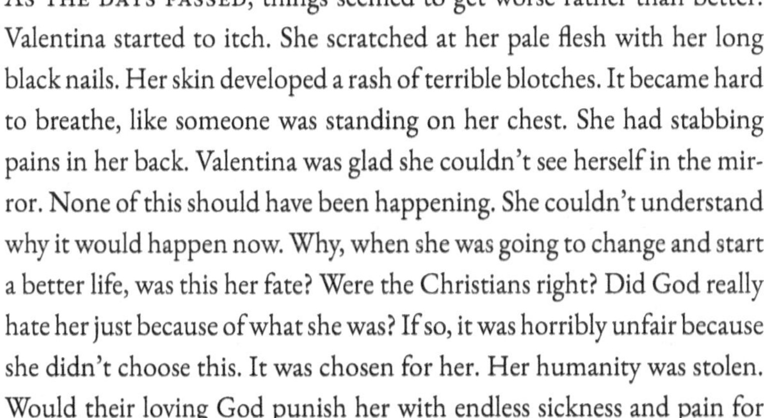

As the days passed, things seemed to get worse rather than better. Valentina started to itch. She scratched at her pale flesh with her long black nails. Her skin developed a rash of terrible blotches. It became hard to breathe, like someone was standing on her chest. She had stabbing pains in her back. Valentina was glad she couldn't see herself in the mirror. None of this should have been happening. She couldn't understand why it would happen now. Why, when she was going to change and start a better life, was this her fate? Were the Christians right? Did God really hate her just because of what she was? If so, it was horribly unfair because she didn't choose this. It was chosen for her. Her humanity was stolen. Would their loving God punish her with endless sickness and pain for being victimized? She didn't know. She had no answers, only questions.

Valentino tried to call Leo and tell him what had transpired, but he wouldn't answer. It was uncharacteristic. Normally, he would have insisted she come to work by now. Maybe he already knew, though she couldn't imagine how. He was going to fire her when he found out, anyway.

One Thursday, Dr. Marlow called and said he had found someone she needed to meet and talk with. She agreed to a rendezvous at the coffee shop on East 8th St. She dressed to cover her rash, but it didn't stop her from feeling like a monster when she entered. She felt like everyone was staring at her. It may have been true since that was nothing new for her, but she knew it may have also been in her head. She felt gross and expected others to see her that way. It was her depression and self-loathing that had driven the vehicle of her life thus far.

Valentina ordered cold tea. Hot beverages hurt her throat too much. The Aids had caused esophagitis. When she had her drink in hand, she turned and saw a man sitting by the window. At least, she assumed it was a man. He was so frail, little more than bones. His skin was ghost-white and full of veins and arteries scrawled all over it like a child's wild art. His eyes were sunken and hollow, his cheekbones sharp, and he wore a headscarf. Valentina took a deep breath and made her way over to him. "Collin?"

"Yes. Please sit," he said in a barely audible voice that still managed to be hoarse. Valentina took a seat.

"Thank you for seeing me," she said.

"I had to," he said. Each word seemed like labor. "No treatments work. It eats away at you like an untreated mortal, but you never die, you get to the brink of death, and you continue on in agony... forever. I've been sick for twenty years, Valentina. It is the worst pain of my life. It is lonely. It is a prison of sickness that someone... like us... cannot escape from."

Valentina sipped her drink to wet her dry mouth. "So what? You came here to tell me there's no hope? You came here to say I should just give up?"

"I came here to say... I don't want you or anyone to go through what I have. To let you know that you have limited time of strength left. Use it. Enjoy what life you can before the sickness won't let you enjoy anything. Don't waste that time on futile treatments that only work on mortals and realize too late that your time is up. Please."

"This is really it?" she asked. "There's nothing else? It's just... done?"

"I'm sorry."

Valentino left the coffee shop and stepped out into the night. The air was cold, and she felt ill. She doubled over and puked in a bush before collapsing to her knees.

"Hey, you okay?" someone asked.

"Fine," she lied. She let them pass and got to her feet, continuing on. Her alarms went off when she saw someone lying in the grass just off the curb. They weren't lying like a sleeping homeless person. They were face down; arms spread like they were hurt. Valentine broke into a run.

She reached them and fell into the grass beside them. She recognized the boy at once. "No, no, no, no," she said, rolling him over.

He looked up at her and blinked. Blood ran from his lips down his chin. It made her heart thrum with the hunger inside her and she hated herself for it. "What happened?" she asked him.

"You made me wait too long," he said weakly.

"I'm so sorry," Valentine said, cradling the boy in her arms. Tears ran down her pale, blotchy cheeks. "I've been sick. I didn't mean to take so long."

"Car... hit me... drove away."

Valentina cursed. "What kind of car? Do you remember?"

"Blue... big.... Cadillac, I think..."

His words faded away. She could feel his heartbeat getting weaker. Valentina shook. She was filled with so much sadness and rage. The boy was dying. She could have saved him before she got sick. She could have given him her blood and healed him, but her blood wouldn't heal him now. It would make him sick, hurt his immune system, and kill him in a different way. She didn't know what vampire Aids would do to a human child, but she knew it wouldn't be good.

Valentina did the only thing she could do. She held the boy close and snuggled him to her chest. She kissed his head, and she asked God to give him peace and a heaven full of rich people truffles and hot showers, and not to punish him for His hatred of her. By the time her prayer was finished, so was the boy. Valentina held him a while longer and cried over him.

Eventually, she laid him gently in the grass and kissed his filthy, blood-streaked face one last time. Then she stood and started walking again. The sickness and pain didn't ebb, but she no longer cared, no longer gave it the power she had before. She had a purpose now. She wouldn't have gotten sick if a sick person was not allowed to fuck her on set. She wouldn't have lost her chance to change her life. She would have been able to save the boy and give him the life he deserved; the life denied to him since birth.

Valentina walked until she reached the warehouse that hid the movie set. She spent so much of her life at. She typed the code in and entered the door. Carmine was seated at his desk, as always. It seemed like he never went home or slept.

"Valentina," he said, failing to mask his surprise.

"Someone on set was sick. Everyone is supposed to be tested," she said, trembling with anger. "The people from my last shoot... were they not tested?"

Carmine nervously flipped through the pages of a notebook. "Um...uh... no, no. It says they were tested. Yes, all tested. All safe."

"Who does the testing?"

"What?"

"You heard the question. Answer it."

"Spencer does it. He's got a spot. I'll write down directions, draw you a map."

"Do it."

Valentina waited for him to do as he said. When he tore the paper from his notebook and handed it to her, she took it and nodded. He was visibly shaking, petrified of her. He had never acted this way before. She stared at him. "What aren't you telling me? What's your part in this?"

"Please. We're friends," he said.

Valentina had heard enough. She let her fangs grow. Then she launched forward, grabbed Carmine by the throat, and lifted him into the air, where she sank those fangs into his jugular. Carmine screamed and kicked, bucked in her grasp, but she held him firm. She ripped with her teeth and tore the meat from his neck, spitting it at the wall where it slapped the peeling paint like the sound of sex. She slurped from the man's resources until his struggles slowed and ceased. Valentina felt stronger. She knew it wouldn't last and the sickness would regain control soon enough, but it would last long enough for her to do what she needed to. She slammed Carmine's lifeless body into the ground hard enough to shatter his bones and carve his skull inward. Then she held the paper in her grip and marched on.

Valentina made it to the makeshift clinic pop tent for porn stars, and she scoffed at it. The people like her, the people she acted with, were treated like they were lesser. They deserved better than this. Just the sight of the place brought her anger to a rising tidal wave, ready to crash down and destroy what was before it. Valentina pushed her way into the tent.

"Hey! What the hell are you doing?" Spencer yelled.

"Shut up. My last shoot, you signed off that all the tests were done and everyone was clean, but someone wasn't, someone got me sick."

"Can I go?" a shirtless adonis said.

"Stay right fucking there," Valentina told him, pointing with a long black fingernail.

"I did my job, Queen," Spencer said, swallowing a lump in his throat. "I'm sorry if you're upset about it."

"Let me see the results. All of them."

"I can't do that. It's illegal."

Valentina was still staring into Spencer's fearful eyes when her right arm lashed out and slashed those black nails across his patient's throat. There was a gurgling and the handsome shirtless man grabbed at his neck, hoping to ebb the tide. It spilled between his fingers and ran down his chiseled torso, coating his muscles in crimson-like strawberry syrup over an ice cream cone. He fell from the chair to his knees, choking on his own blood. Valentina never so much as looked over at him. She just listened to him die as she stared into Spencer's eyes. "Now."

"Yes, Queen." Spencer got up in a hurry and knocked his stool over. He went to a filing cabinet and rustled through it frantically, fumbling with trembling fingers. Valentina sat in the dying man's seat. He continued to choke and spasm at her feet. A lightning-quick hand grabbed him from the floor and pulled him to her lips. She drank of him while she watched Spencer look for the paperwork.

"Here. It's here," he said, turning back towards her with a handful of parchment. Valentina flicked her wrist and launched the man she held into the wall of the pop-up tent. The force of his impact ripped the canvas and sent him sprawling to the concrete on the other side. Spencer stared at the hole, his eyes wide and glistening with tears of terror.

Valentina wiped her mouth and looked at the papers. It was the lab results on the blood tests. Her eyes tightened with anger, and she held one paper up, dropping the rest. "Him? Alan? The reason Leo wouldn't let me go home? If I had, I would be able to live, to find love, to save that boy."

"What boy, Queen?"

"It doesn't matter now. What do you do with these test results?"

"I...I... I give them to Henry. He's Leo's guy. I don't know what happens after that. I'm sorry."

Valentina had fire burning in her eyes when she glared at him. "Tell me where to find them both."

"What?"

Valentina leapt to her feet and shot across the tent, grabbing him by his shirt. Immediately, his pants darkened, and a stream of urine ran out his pant leg onto the floor. "Tell me where to find Alan and where to find Henry. Now."

"Y-Yes, Queen. Just... please, but me down."

Valentina dropped him. In a blur of motion that seemed like a gust of winter wind, she was back in her seat.

The trembling man sat back down himself, forgetting his stool had toppled and he fell to the floor. Valentina huffed at this. "Today, Spencer."

"Right," he said, scrambling to his feet. He grabbed his laptop and started typing. "Are you going to kill me?"

"Are you going to give me what I ask for?"

"Y-yes, of course." he typed some more, moved the mouse around, and continued typing. "Here. Here," he said, turning the laptop around so she could see it. The glowing screen had a list of employees' names, addresses, and phone numbers.

"Print it."

"I - I don't have a printer. But I can email it to you."

"I can do that myself," she said. Before he could ask the question on his lips, her teeth were ripping his lips from his face. He screamed as the teeth darted back towards his nose. Hands grasped at what was left of his face and he fell screaming to the floor as Valentina spit his nose out. Spencer was sobbing on the floor when Valentina's black leather high-heeled boot lifted high and came down on the back of his head. The force of the blow was enough to carry her momentum straight through and his skull exploded, leaving her boot on the ground in a pile of gore. Her eyes were on the laptop. She sent an email to herself and then turned and walked out of the rip in the tent.

VALENTINA COULD SEE HENRY through the window. He was sitting at a computer desk, masturbating to whatever was on the screen. She shook her head and used a black fingernail still crusted with blood to pick the lock on his door. When it came open silently, she slipped in and moved through the shadows. A moment later, she was behind his chair, whispering into his ear as he tugged hard at his manhood.

"You like porn?"

Henry shivered and slid down in his chair, then jumped up. "What the fuck?" he cried out, his voice cracking like a child going through puberty.

When Valentina saw the screen, she laughed. "Is that me? Are you jerking off to me, Henry?"

Henry looked back at his computer and quickly fumbled to shut the monitor off. He looked back at her. "What are you doing here?"

"That's a good question, Henry. Put your dick away. I have no desire to see any more of those."

He nodded and flushed pink, shoving his hard-on back into his pants and zipping them around it. It still bulged through the fabric, but it was better, she thought.

"Spencer came to you with test results, results that showed Alan was HIV positive, and somehow he still managed to fuck me."

Henry swallowed hard. "I gave those results to Leo. It's his call, you know. I just pass on the information. He said you would be okay because you're a vamp. He said shit like that couldn't affect you."

"He was wrong, and you can't put it all on him when you knew and you were the one that came to get me for that shoot. You came to get me and led me to a man that would ruin my life and the life of an innocent boy. You did so willingly."

"I couldn't say anything. I would have been fired."

"Fired." Valentina laughed. "That would have been a worse fate than this? I changed my mind. Take it back out."

"What?"

"You heard me. Take it out."

"N-uh no, I don't want to."

"I didn't ask what you wanted, like you didn't ask me. Do as I say as you did what Leo said. That's what you're good at, isn't it? Following orders? If you don't, I will open your throat like an envelope."

Henry looked at her. He seemed to be contemplating, thinking it through. He swallowed again and then slowly reached down and unzipped his pants. In a blur of movement, Valentina had his cock in her undead hand. It stiffened again at her touch. She looked into his eyes as she pulled it down like a lever. There was a loud snapping like the branch of a tree had been broken in too and Henry fell to the floor screaming.

"I'm going to kill you," she said. "Just like you killed me. Then I'm going to kill Alan, and last but certainly not least, I'm going to kill Leo. I hope it was worth it for whatever money you made."

Henry was in a fetal position, holding his broken dick and sobbing. Valentine used one of her boots to roll him onto his back. She slid down over him, straddling him at the waist. "Please," he whimpered.

"It's too late for that." Valentina's hands came one after another, back and forth, moving fast enough to create trails as her nails ripped and tore at his mid-section. Blood spattered in every direction and soaked the room. When he was an open shell of mutilated organs, she stood. Valentina turned the monitor back on and saw his blood dripping down her naked form. She left it like that when she ran back out into the night.

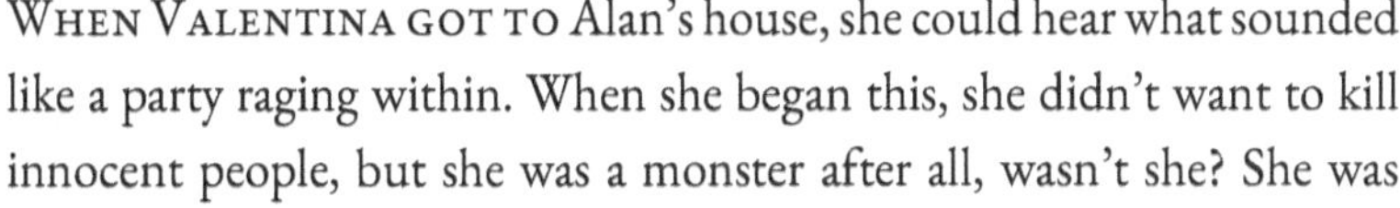

WHEN VALENTINA GOT TO Alan's house, she could hear what sounded like a party raging within. When she began this, she didn't want to kill innocent people, but she was a monster after all, wasn't she? She was what everyone made her into, what they all wanted her to be, and her time was limited.

She didn't bother with the door. Valentina dove through the window. It shattered around her and she tumbled into a roll and bounded to her feet. There were four people in the hallway. She took all their throats and ran into the kitchen. Several people were drinking and laughing. They fell silent when she entered. She whirled around the room, tearing, biting, and smashing them one by one. She drank of their resources and left their bodies draped over the table, chairs, and kitchen counter. Then she moved further into the house. She found some people dancing in the living room. They didn't hear her over the music, and she raced in behind them. By the time someone finally started to scream, the others had all been decapitated. The scream was stopped short by a vampiric hand punching through their teeth and seizing their tongue. She ripped the muscle out of their face and threw it to the ground to lay among the scattered pieces of ivory her fist had broken through in order to retrieve it. The woman started to fall, but Valentina pinned her to the wall with a heel in her throat. She pushed that heel until it hit the wall and the head above toppled off onto the floor with the rest.

She left the music playing and continued through the house. She found a girl snorting coke off the toilet seat in the bathroom. Valentina grabbed her by the hair and smashed her face into the porcelain repeatedly. With each hit, more blood came free and more of the toilet chipped away. Then there were bone fragments and bits of brain toppling from her destroyed face. Valentina dropped her face down into the toilet and went back to the hall.

She made it to the bedroom in the back and paused. She could hear the moans of ecstasy that accompanied sex coming from the other side of the door. She slipped the door open slowly and quietly and then peered through the opening. Alan was on his back amid a pile of silk sheets with a tanned brunette riding him. She whipped her hair around and moaned as her hips rocked back and forth. The sight of him having sex when he knew he was positive filled Valentina with a fury like nothing she had ever known. She roared and charged into the room.

Alan sat up just as Valentina's fist broke through the woman's chest cavity and came out right before his face. He reacted and vomited over her naked breasts. Valentina tugged her hand in reverse out the woman's back. She held a beating heart in her hand as Alan's sex partner slumped to those shining sheets. Valentina stood before him. She approached the side of the bed where she could reach his face and she bit into the heart like an apple as she went.

Alan said nothing. Unlike the others, he didn't plead for his life. He didn't claim to be innocent or pass the buck onto someone else. He just watched her silently and waited. He must have known he was guilty. "Did you tell her?" Valentina asked, leaning over by his face. "You didn't tell me."

Alan still failed to speak. She reached with one hand and pried his mouth open like a trapdoor. Her other hand shoved his mate's half-eaten heart into his mouth. He mumbled something then and tears came out of his eyes to run down his cheeks. Valentina worked his jaw for him, forcing him to chew the dead woman's organ. Blood squirted from between his teeth and ran down his chin. She leaned over and licked it off his face.

She grabbed the body of the dead woman then and lifted her off of him, tossing her to the side like a sack of laundry. His cock remained as giant and painful as she remembered. She slashed a black nail from its base, up its shaft to the head, opening it wide and splitting the veins within. The blood ran free, and the giant member slowly went limp and draped over like a slab of wet celery. "Not so impressive anymore, is it?"

Alan started to gag and spit out the chewed-up heart. Valentina plunged her hand into his belly. It broke through just like the man broke through the tent at her last stop. She kept going and reached her arm up through him. It pushed out through the flesh like a baby writhing within, the baby she would never get to have. Then, when her arm was inside him all the way to the shoulder, she ripped it free. Flesh exploded and blood sprayed the wall above the bed in a rainbow arc. He collapsed with a frozen wide-eyed stare, and she left him there to go visit her boss. It was time for Valentina to get her severance pay.

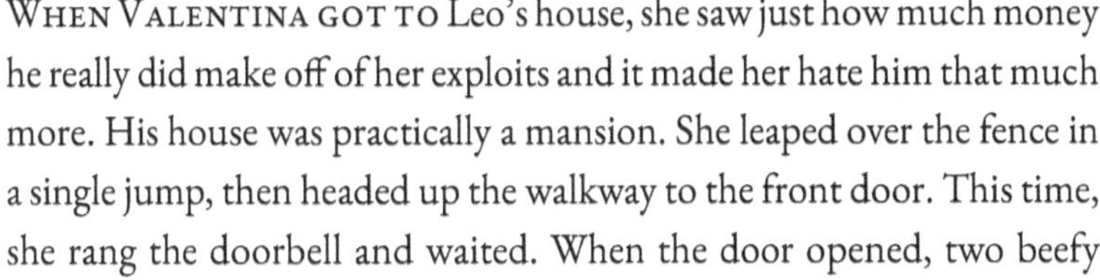

WHEN VALENTINA GOT TO Leo's house, she saw just how much money he really did make off of her exploits and it made her hate him that much more. His house was practically a mansion. She leaped over the fence in a single jump, then headed up the walkway to the front door. This time, she rang the doorbell and waited. When the door opened, two beefy armed guards stood before her. "You can't be here," one of them said.

Valentina took the left one's throat with a single swipe as she leapt onto the right one. She wrapped her legs around his waist and sank her fangs into his neck. He stumbled around, trying to get free of her. He punched at her wildly, but she wouldn't budge. When he had been drained enough that he fell to his knees, only then did she jump off. She grabbed his head with both hands and twisted, snapping his neck with a crunch. Before he hit the floor, she was down the hall.

She spotted Leo in a room to the right. It had a crackling fire in a fireplace and two recliners. Leo stood before the left one, sipping from a martini glass, green olive floating in the clear liquid within. "Val baby, my Queen," he said when she entered. "You don't look so good. Come sit down and rest. I'll get you a drink."

"Fuck you," she said back.

"Now, is that any way to talk to your friend? Come on. We made a lot of money together. I made you. You helped make me. We're in this thing together, right?"

"Wrong. I am done...with everything. You let Alan screw me when you knew he was positive."

Leo sighed. He raised his arms up defensively. "What did you want me to do? Word was already going around that you were trying to quit on me, Val."

"So, you did it on purpose? To what? Teach me a lesson?"

"No. Come on. I thought it wouldn't affect you. I thought vamps would be immune to shit like that. I didn't think Aids would take down the Queen of Dark desires. I just knew time was running out, and I needed to finish this film before I had an unfinished movie and a star who wouldn't do it."

He started to walk through the house, and she followed him, watching him and listening, in no hurry to finish him. "So, you were just in a rush to finish your film before I quit."

"Exactly, Val. Come on, baby. You're my queen. I wouldn't have done it if I didn't think you'd be okay."

"I'm not okay, Leo."

He continued to lead her through the house. He opened a door and went through it. She flew forward to make sure she didn't lose him and realized they were in a garage. "You don't really think you're getting away, do you?"

"Come on, Val. It was an honest mistake."

She saw the car he was trying to get into, and her eyes widened. It was a blue Cadillac with blood still on the fender and grill. The keyless entry beeped as the door unlocked with a click. "It was you," she said. "You killed the boy."

Leo opened the driver's side door. He stopped and looked at her over it. "I had no choice, my Queen. He filled your head with nonsense. He made you want to quit. You're my bread and butter. He stole that from me. I thought with him gone, you would come back to me. I thought you would be okay, and we would just go back to how things were and make money together."

Valentina didn't even roar. She was too angry to scream. Her rage was a tangible thing, a weapon. She moved unseen, crossing the garage, and slammed the car door on him. He cried out. When she opened it, he let his legs go limp and slid to the floor, rolling underneath the vehicle.

Valentina peered underneath and saw him squirting out the other side. She stood and jumped ina single movement, landing on top of the car with a thump. Leo was pounding the button on a remote and the garage door was slowly opening. Valentina dove forward, spiraling like a screwdriver. She crashed into him and took him with her through the moving garage door into the gravel driveway.

"I've always had your best interests in mind, Val. Come on. You're my Queen, right? Everything I did, I did for you."

She didn't say anything back. She just grabbed his arms, one with each hand, and she ripped in opposite directions. Leo came apart in her grip. His body tore in half and all that was left was a spine and a rib cage in a puddle of gore with a heart beating within. Valentina took the heart with her. She bit into it and ate as she walked.

Valentina walked to the park. The body of the poor dead homeless boy remained where she left him. People really just didn't care about his kind, no more than they cared about hers. There wasn't much left of the night. She needed to make use of the moments she had. She laid down on the grass beside the boy and wrapped him in her arms once more. "I'm sorry," she said. "I'm so sorry."

Valentina lay there, holding the dead child, feeling the grass on her skin, and she waited for the sun to rise.

4

QUEEN OF HEARTS

BY NAT WHISTON

IN THE DARKNESS OF a desolate street, inside an abandoned house, the only sound that can be heard are the screams of pain from a young woman. Something stirs in the garden, waiting and looking up from the outside, at the battered and broken remains of the upstairs bedroom. Peter Ashworth takes his wife's hand and tries to calm her as she sobs.

"I know it hurts, baby, but it shouldn't be long now," Peter whispered.

Tears rush down her cheeks as the pain overloads her senses. She wants this all to be over. They have been on the run for months since they got the news. Peter kissed her forehead and started to hum a tune to calm her. Nothing was working, but Peter was at a loss as he had never been through this before. Ever since the World changed and the new queen had crossed into their reality, nothing was normal.

Every subtle noise made him jumpy; he knew by now her screams would have attracted unwanted attention. When they arrived in the area, it looked deserted, but there was no way they could be sure. The new queen has spies everywhere, hunting down those that had been picked for selection. When the news reached the queen of Mrs Ashworth's change of status, they became fugitives.

His wife let out another howl of pain, snapping Peter from his thoughts. The sound echoed through the building, rattling off the walls until it was deafening.

"Gag me," she begged, with a vice-like grip on his arm.

"What?"

"We can't risk being discovered, the pain…" she paused to take a breath. "I can't control my reactions. You need to gag me."

Peter nodded. He never dreamed that this was a request he would carry out. On his wife no less, but desperate times call for desperate measures. He tore a piece of lining and wrapped it around her head, with the knot tied in the centre for her to bite down on, just in time for the next contraction, and her teeth slammed down on the taut material.

"I am so sorry, darling," he sobbed, gently running his fingers through her hair.

Strands of sweat-matted hair clung to her face, which he carefully pushed aside; he looked down the length of her body. His eyes widen in horror when he sees the bottom of her dress soaked in fresh blood.

He quickly crawled to the source of the bleeding and tentatively pulled up her skirt. He wasn't prepared for this, but he should have been. He read all the books weeks in advance and stole what he needed from the hospitals to be prepared. But as Peter yanked rolls and rolls of gauze from his rucksack, he realised they would not be enough. He reached his hand under her skirt, closing his eyes tight as he reached inside her.

Shit, she's fully dilated. It's time.

Peter's adrenaline finally kicked in and he rushed to his feet and headed downstairs praying that he would find a gas stove. It seemed his prayers had been answered when he saw the metal pot on top of the steel ring. He grabbed the pot and turned the tap, no water.

"Fuck."

He checked the cupboards and found a bottle of water, frantically unscrewing the top and tipping it into the metal pot. He felt eyes on the back of his neck as he clicked the button while turning the dial. The flame burst upwards and started to heat up the water within. While he waited for the water to boil, he ran into the bathroom to get towels. Peter tucked them under his arm and poured the water with the other into a bowl. Just about to leave the room, a chill ran down his spine. Something in the pit of his stomach knew something was wrong. He turned slowly toward the window, and a shadowy figure eclipsed the glass. The shock almost made him drop the pot of water, but he regained his composure. He steadied his breathing and placed the water on the side, looking back at the window.

No sign of the mysterious figure.

Peter still can't shake that feeling in his gut, warning him of an unseen danger. He hears a muffled cry above him and remembers his wife, alone upstairs. He rushes over to the bowl and grabs it, doing everything he cannot to spill its contents. As he hurried towards the stairs with towels under his arms, he heard the wind whistle through the cracks in the walls.

They would have to leave soon.

Anxious, he made it to the top of the stairs and turned into the bedroom. His wife was on all fours, screaming into her gag as blood poured from between her legs.

This is not how they imagined bringing their child into the world, not by a long shot. Peter fell to his knees, dunking towels into the water bowl now by his side. Her bowels had released, and shit coated the back of her legs as she moved into a squat. Her hand gripping the bedsheets so hard her nails begin to bleed. [CN1] Compared to what she was going through, the blood dripping from his palm was nothing.

"You need to push Alice. It's time. Push baby," Peter urged.

Through a stream of tears, she lets out a muffled sob and starts to tense her body. He rests the hot towel on her back. He would rather she be having an epidural for the pain. But they couldn't risk a hospital, he knew Alice and him would be found. Someone would no doubt recognize them from the media or news reports. In her condition, there was no way that they would escape before dark, so this was the only option. Trying to hide away until morning, but when her water broke at the doorway, Peter knew it was game over. Alice was strong, but there was no way she could travel after such a taxing event.

He watched as Alice closed her eyes tight and put every bit of her energy into the last push. Peter heard a sickening squelching noise as the baby exited its mother and landed on the cushion of blankets underneath.

Blood was everywhere and Alice was incredibly weak, but even in her dazed state, something forced her to look back, and she yanked the gag from her mouth.

"Peter, she's not crying."

He rushed from her side to the newborn, still covered in gore, but silent as the grave. Alice collapsed onto her side and reached out weakly for her child.

"Give her to me, Pete," Alice pleads.

Her pleas go unanswered as Peter focuses his full attention on their baby. Swaddling her in warm towels, he begins to rub her back, hoping and praying that she lets out her first cry.

Alice begins to sob as the longest moment of their lives continues when their bundle of joy refuses to cry out.

That is when Alice notices a shape in the window.

"Peter."

"Give me a moment, Alice," he snapped, still trying to pull their child back into this world.

Alice's eyes focus hard on the dark mass covering the window, blocking out the lights from the street. Peter's heart was pounding in his ears now, as he desperately tried to revive their daughter.

Just as Peter was losing hope, the tiny infant let out a wail. He couldn't believe how happy he was to hear such a shrill, high-pitched cry. She had some lungs on her for sure, no doubt taking after her mother.

He finally turned his attention to Alice. The smile beaming on his face was soon diminished when he noticed the terrified look in her eyes.

"Alice,"

She didn't respond.

"Ali? Are you ok?"

Finally, she acknowledged his presence as the trance over her was broken. Her eyes filled with tears as Peter handed her their daughter, and she kissed the little girl on the forehead. She held her close to her bare chest as Peter sat behind her to support her. For the first time in months, everything felt normal. Just a mother holding her baby while the father sat behind her, beaming with pride. A perfect moment.

Until it was shattered by the sounds of breaking glass.

Peter shot up from behind Alice and grabbed the baseball bat by the wall. He would protect his family, no matter what.

"ALICE TAKE THE BABY AND HIDE!"

"But Peter…"

"There's no time, just do it!" Peter commanded.

With no further words spoken between them, she rose to her feet and wandered over to the wardrobe at the back. The sound of heavy footsteps coming up the stairs made Alice hurry inside. The baby had stopped crying but was still fussing. Alice could tell she was hungry. She watched through a crack in the wardrobe as soldiers wearing burgundy entered the room and surrounded Peter. He stood proudly, bat in hand as they raised their weapons at his head.

From the back of the circle, a large, cloaked figure wandered into the room and faced Peter.

"Where is she?" the hooded figure asked.

"Far away by now," Peter snapped.

The figure looked around the room, and when his attention fell on the bloody sheets, Peter held back his panic.

"Not in her current condition," He scoffed, before resting a hand on one of the shoulders of the soldiers. "Tear the place apart."

The command tore through Peter, as fear engulfed him.

I must protect my family.

That one thought gave him all the adrenaline and drive he needed, and he lunged at the men heading towards the wardrobe. He punched one of the men, but it didn't shift the monster of a man. In response, the man in red camouflage simply headbutted Peter, knocking him flying to the ground, dazed and unable to see the next attack coming. A swift kick to the ribs knocked the wind out of Peter as he gasped for air.

He hears the doors to the wardrobe open, stuck to the ground, unable to move. He lay helpless on the wooden floor as they dragged Alice out, clutching in her arms their screaming baby. He could hear her crying. But the sound is muffled. Everything is still blurry from the collision with the larger man, who now stood leering down at him, gun pointing at his temple. All he can do is watch on the ground; the barrel pinned against his head. Alice is held by her throat, and they yanked the baby girl from her grasp.

"No, please, not my baby! Give me back my baby!" Alice wailed.

"Please...not our baby," Peter begged.

The soldier above him sneered and turned back toward Alice and forced her to her knees. The cloaked figure loomed over her, dagger in hand, the sharp tip glistened in the moonlight.

"Alice Ashworth, you have been charged with treason to the crown. How do you plead?"

"Not guilty! Please give her back to me!"

"But did you, or did you not flee before your trial before the crowned queen?"

"That monster is not my queen," Alice barked.

The soldiers stepped backward as tension collected in the air. All the guards that surrounded her were silent for a moment.

The cloaked figure pulled away their hood, revealing a middle-aged man. His thick black hair flowed past his shoulders and his dark black eyes pierced through Peter. Before turning his attention back to Alice, who was now being bound by the man holding her in place.

"You must be the one," He whispered. The gaunt man bent down to look into her eyes.

Peter began to shake; he could not control his nerves as the man motioned to the soldiers holding his wife in place. One exits the room, and another holds a tight grip on both of Alice's shoulders. The baby started to cry as she was placed to the side in a discarded cardboard box.

"Please, let me hold her! Let me hold my daughter!" Peter called to the soldier.

"QUIET, TRAITOR!"

The large soldier's booming voice almost deafened him as he leaned down, yelling into his ear. Another sharp whack to the head with the butt of the gun, and Peter was forced into submission once again. Blood poured down from the cut above his eyebrow and through the crimson blur, he could see his wife's pained expression. He looked down to see a puddle of blood around her knees. The bleeding hadn't stopped since she gave birth, and her face was turning pale.

"Please, my wife has just given birth. She needs a doctor."

Silence. Not one person in the room even acknowledged his pleas.

"What the hell is wrong with you? Can't you see she needs help!" panic lifted the volume of his tone.

"Silence!" The sharp command came from the doorway.

Peter cannot believe his eyes.

The bitch decided to show up personally.

Even though his vision was still swimming, he had seen enough photos and newspapers to know what the Red Queen looked like. In the flesh, she was even more terrifying.

Her deep red eyes looked straight through him as a cold burst of air chilled him to the bone.

Everything from her hair to her outfit was perfectly presented, not a crease to be seen in the valour dress that caressed her figure. Nothing was out of place; the silk shawl was blood-red, and her boots climbed up to the knee. Her makeup was perfectly detailed, a heavy shade of burgundy on a background of porcelain skin. No one would ever think that such a beauty would be such a cruel and hateful woman. Peter couldn't help wondering why she was here, out in the middle of nowhere in the shittiest part of England. In the dead of night, to what? Simply come to pass judgment herself. No, it was more than that. She had come to collect in person, and Peter's veins ran cold. He knew what was coming next.

"Please, your Majesty, spare my wife. I promise she is not the one you seek!"

Blood and tears mixed as he strained to move, but the behemoth of a man had him locked in place.

"How dare you address the Queen!" the cloaked man spat.

"Show some respect for your Queen, traitor!" Another soldier yelled.

"Please my Queen, we have a child! Have mercy," Peter grovelled.

"Peter, don't," Alice wept.

He stopped struggling and looked deep into her eyes. She looked so fragile. It was taking all her strength just to hold up her head, in that moment, it was clear to Peter.

She was dying anyway.

He stopped struggling and focused all his attention on her, the way her hair fell to the side. The gentle way she rested her hand on his when she slept, every smile line and freckle. Like it was the last time.

Because it was.

Alice turned away from him and faced the Queen. Her ruby-red eyes looked deep into Alice's; Peter had noticed the once vivid blue of her iris was slowly fading to a grey hue. Dark circles rested under her eyes as life continued to pour out beneath her. The Queen turned her attention to the scarlet puddle beneath his wife and smiled wickedly.

"Truly sorry about this, my dear, but you understand," the Queen's voice trails off slightly as she reaches behind her.

"Yes, your ma..." Alice's sentence comes to an abrupt stop as the dagger plunges into the side of her throat.

Peter sat on the ground, shocked, as Alice turned her head to him. Her eyes were wide with fear. She couldn't scream as the blade had gone straight through her vocal cords. Alice's eyes rolled into her head, and she fell backward onto the floor. Blood spurted in all directions from the massive gash in her throat. The Queen simply wiped the blade on her dress and handed it back to the man in the cloak.

Alice lay lifeless on the ground in front of him, and the grief consumed him. Peter let out a mournful cry that rang out through the dishevelled structure. The man holding him down used all his strength to keep the grieving husband face down on the floor. Peter had to watch as the cloaked man knelt over his wife's body. He heard the sickening sound of metal piercing bone, and the soldier turned his head to the side, forcing

Peter to watch helplessly on the ground as his baby called out for her mother, while the man began sawing through her chest bone. Peter could hear the vile noise the saw made as it cut back and forth through Alice's sternum. Peter wanted to be sick. the sound of his wife's chest being cracked open made his stomach flip. But he should have expected this. They both heard the rumours they just didn't want to believe it was true.

Finally, inside her open chest cavity, the man reaches inside Alice's corpse. With both hands, he carefully lifted out the heart of Peter's beloved. Raising it above his head, the residual blood trickled down his gloved hands. The Queen reached down and took it in both hands and held it in front of her, examining every section of the now lifeless organ. The smile leaves her lips and is replaced by a look of disappointment.

"It's not her," she comments.

A box is brought over to her by a tall gentleman. The contrast of his ebony skin and the vivid red suit seemed very out of place. Especially with the scene of gore and violence that plagued the floor, Peter was pinned against.

"It will do for the collection," she confirmed, dismissing him with a wave of her bloody hand.

"I'm so sorry, Your Highness, I was so sure it was her," the cloaked man lowered his head in penance.

"No matter Percival, the real Alice cannot hide from me forever. We will get the right one eventually. I mean, all those named Alice have been arrested or are currently being removed."

"True. I have seen to it that the borders and transport out of England have been closed off, so it's not like she can leave this tiny island," he scoffed.

"She will rue the day she stepped foot in my domain," The Queen threatened, with a smirk.

Peter lay on the ground, a beaten excuse for a man now. Having watched the woman he loved be mutilated before his very eyes. The Queen's attention turns to a mewing sound at the edge of the room, reawakening Peter's basic instincts.

"What about the child, your majesty?"

She wandered over to the box which housed the infant and sneered at the bundle before she turned and headed back towards the doorway.

Peter let out a sigh of relief.

She abruptly stopped at the threshold and turned on her heels, looking Peter dead in the eyes. A smile crept across her lips as she then looked at one of the soldiers. Her hand reaching for something at his side. Peter froze.

"On second thoughts..."

Peter's mind began to scream at him to get up as terror bolted through his body.

But before he could react, a gun barrel was placed against his forehead and the Red Queen loomed over him.

"...I do believe *that* particular heart is missing from my collection."

His world ended with the sound of a bang, mixed with the terrified cries of his daughter...

5

— • —

HEAVY IS THE HEAD THAT WEARS THE CROWN

BY TARA LOSACANO

CASEY SMILED AT HER reflection, her red dress sparkling in the lamplight. Tonight was the night she'd been waiting her entire life for. It was prom night. Casey Stiles had been envisioning her prom since she was just a small girl. Now eighteen, and on the cusp of womanhood, she felt her dreams coming true.

Tonight, she would be named Prom Queen. Casey had no doubt that she would be winning the crown. Well, maybe the tiniest bit of doubt. Her opponent, Celeste Matthews, was the school's most popular girl, next to Casey, of course. Celeste was not only beautiful, but she was also kind and genuine. Casey hated her. She was beautiful herself, but Celeste had the flowing blonde hair and pale skin that Casey had always yearned for. But no, Casey had naturally black hair, olive skin, and dark eyes. She could never pull off blonde.

As she did one more quick twirl in the mirror, admiring the way her dress spun with her, her mom yelled up from downstairs, letting her know that her boyfriend Robbie had arrived.

"Oh my, you look so handsome, Robert." her mother swooned over her boyfriend, who looked rather dapper in his black tux and tie.

As she cleared the landing, both her mother and Robbie turned and gaped at her.

"Oh my God, Casey. You look amazing." Robbie said, the sincerity evident.

"You look so beautiful, honey!" her mom exclaimed loudly.

"Thank you. And you look great, Robbie." she said with a slight smile. She and Rob had been together for just six months, their relationship starting to grow more intense. Casey did care for him, but she wasn't in love with him. She did, however, think he was going to make the perfect Prom King.

As she walked over, he pulled the red corsage from its package and held it out for her to slip onto her wrist. He had made sure to ask what color dress she'd be wearing so the flower could match. Casey had purposely chosen the color red. She knew Celeste was planning to wear a white dress, and Casey wanted to make sure she stood out. Besides, didn't people say red was viewed as sexy? She couldn't remember.

After fixing the corsage and pinning Robbie's boutonniere onto his jacket, Casey's mother took a few photos while gushing over how amazing they both looked. When Casey finally convinced her mom she'd taken enough pictures, they started towards the front door.

"Oh Casey, I'm sorry, could I just steal you for one quick minute in the kitchen? Sorry, Robert. Just one moment," her mom said and then slipped her arm through Casey's to walk to the other room.

Once out of earshot, Casey's mom said, "Cass, I meant to ask earlier but completely forgot what with the excitement. You took your medication, right?" Her eyes watched Casey closely.

"Yeah mom, I took it. All set." Casey answered, knowing she wasn't being truthful.

"Good girl. Okay, you have fun and don't forget if anything happens or you need me, you just call. You're going to be crowned Prom Queen tonight, I just know it!"

Robbie opened the passenger door and Casey very carefully swept her dress to the side and got in. Watching him come around the front of the car, Casey felt a rush of pride. Robbie was good looking and popular; she just knew he was going to make the best prom king. Tonight was just going to be perfect. It had to be. First, she'd win her crown and be titled Prom Queen. Then she'd lose her virginity to Robbie afterwards. She'd already planned everything out and nothing was going to ruin her night. An image of Celeste popped into Casey's mind as she thought this, but she quickly shook it away.

They pulled into the parking lot of the fancy banquet hall that had been decorated beautifully for the night's prom. They found a parking spot and Casey waited while Robbie walked over and opened her door for her. Her mind raced, excited that this night had finally arrived. It was the night she would show everybody that she was worthy of being crowned queen. She didn't really even like most of her classmates, but she wanted them to admire her.

"You ready?" He asked with a grin on his face.

"Absolutely!" Casey responded. She couldn't wait to get inside so everyone could see how gorgeous she looked in her red dress. Most of the senior girls didn't like Casey, but she just figured it was because they were jealous of her. She didn't go out of her way to be nasty to these girls, but she also didn't waste her time trying to be friendly, either.

As they made their way through the doors, Casey gasped at how beautifully the hall was decorated. There were silver and white streamers and balloons all throughout the spacious area. It was magical. Casey saw that the dance floor was already packed with her classmates, the music blaring. She had a sudden rush of excitement at the thought of standing on the stage at the front of the room and looking down at all her peers as her crown got placed onto her head, accentuating her beautiful, dark hair. She felt Robbie pull her arm a bit, and she began walking again. They found their friends at a nearby table.

"Casey! Oh my God, you look beautiful! Everybody watch out, soon to be Prom Queen coming through," Casey's friend Brianna exclaimed as she ran over and gave Casey a hug. The girls squealed together as the boys shook hands and greeted each other.

"Have you seen Celeste?" Casey whispered to Brianna.

"Not yet. Apparently, she's not here yet, but plans to make a grand entrance." Brianna rolled her eyes.

"Of course, she always needs all the attention to be on her. Well, tonight is MY night." Casey spouted angrily.

"Hey, of course it is. Don't worry, you've got this in the bag," Brianna said soothingly.

As the girls continued to chat, there was a sudden commotion near the entrance and the group looked over. The crowd watched as a white stretch limo stopped directly in front of the grand entrance. Casey already knew it was her rival Celeste inside, and her stomach twisted, making her feel sick.

Celeste's boyfriend, Brian, came from around the other side of the limo and opened the other door. Casey walked closer to the entrance so she could see better. Celeste slowly exited the limo and as she stood, Casey inhaled sharply, as did most of the crowd. She was absolutely stunning. Her white dress almost mimicked a wedding dress but showed a lot more skin. The low-cut neckline exposed Celeste's cleavage, her large breasts an obvious attraction for the guys. But the girls swooned too, wishing to be in Celeste's shoes at that moment. Casey felt her heart sink, and doubt flooded her mind.

Just the thought of Celeste winning prom queen over her filled her with a deep rage and jealousy unlike anything she'd ever felt before. Even worse than the time at her old school when her crush asked her best friend out on a date instead of her. It devastated Casey. But when her best friend happened to get "food poisoning" the night of her date. Casey swooped in and spent the night with her crush instead. She never told anyone that she may have slipped a little something into her friend's food earlier that day.

The crowd opened, making a path for Celeste as she sauntered into the hall, her white dress sparkling, her eyes shining bright with joy. Casey couldn't stand her. And Celeste was heading straight in her direction.

"Hi Casey! Just wanted to say good luck tonight. You look beautiful," Celeste spoke softly and with genuine kindness.

Casey peered at her for a moment and then finally responded coldly, "Thanks, you too."

Everyone at the table watched quietly, feeling the tension coming off of Casey. Brianna finally jumped up to break the awkwardness.

"You look amazing, Celeste. I love your dress! Whoever wins tonight will deserve the title, for sure."

Casey whipped her head around, glaring at her friend. Did she really just say "whoever wins"? Didn't she believe Casey would be winning tonight? Her mind started spiraling, the little seed of doubt now threatening to grow into something bigger. She quickly pushed the thoughts down again.

"Anyway, I'm going to go get some punch, I'll see you guys." Celeste said, giving Brianna a slight hug and walking away with her date. Casey watched, hate burning in her eyes.

"Cass, you okay?" Brianna whispered into her ear, a worried look on her face.

She looked at her friend, and she suddenly seemed like a stranger to her, and for a split second, her face morphed into something hideous and ugly. Casey recoiled, gasping.

"What is it? What's wrong?!" her friend asked. Now Robbie and Briannas date, Chase, were watching them. Casey snapped out of it and immediately apologized to her friend. She had to keep her shit together. Tonight was not the night to let her mind slip.

After getting some punch and sitting to eat, the music really started bumping, and the dance floor was packed. Casey watched as her classmates danced and had fun together. She sat rigidly, waiting impatiently for what she came for. Her crown. That's the only thing that really mattered tonight. She even made a special spot in her room, all ready to show off her crown when she got home. She bought a small, red satin pillow to rest it on. It was going to be perfect.

"Come on, dance with me!" Robbie came over, extending his hand to Casey. As she looked up into his dark eyes, she snapped out of her thoughts. She reminded herself this was supposed to be a fun night, full of memories. Yes, it was about the crown for Casey, but she still wanted to be able to look back on this night fondly. She smiled at Robbie and stood up to walk to the dance floor. They found Brianna and Chase, and the group laughed as they danced together.

Casey moved her body to the music, closing her eyes. She could feel the rhythm of the instruments moving through her. Her mind started drifting and the darkness behind her eyes started filling with red. She quickly opened her eyes and saw directly in her line of sight was Celeste. She was dancing with her date and their friends, looking carefree and happy. Casey's eyes darkened and hate enveloped her once again. Celeste was not better than her, nor was she prettier. She had no chance of winning tonight, Casey told herself, though that seed of doubt still lingered somewhere inside her mind. As she watched, the faces of those around her started to morph into something ugly. The smiles of her classmates suddenly looked sinister.

Casey's eyes darted from peer to peer. Each of them seemed to be glaring back at her, laughing silently.

"Hey, you okay?" Robbie grabbed her hand and Casey jumped.

"Yeah. Yeah, I'm fine," she smiled at him, her eyes swinging back to Celeste as Robbie turned away. Celeste was looking right at her now, and Casey wasn't sure, but it looked like she gave her a wink before turning away and continuing dancing with her friends. Casey looked around at the faces nearby, now looking happy and normal again. Casey knew she couldn't always trust her mind. She was supposed to take medication to keep her steady and to avoid things like this from happening, but she hated it, and rarely actually took it the way she was supposed to. Her mother had tried everything, and Casey had seen many doctors. After a while, she just started telling them what they wanted to hear, so they'd just leave her alone.

"Okay everybody, ladies and gents. Listen up! It's time! The time you've all been waiting for. We're going to announce who won this year's Prom King and Prom Queen!!" the principal, Mrs.Hibbert, stood on stage with her microphone, grinning stupidly.

Casey gasped and almost stumbled. It was time, finally. Her crown would be placed on her head and the entire school would finally know she was the queen.

"Cass, it's time!!" Brianna ran over next to her and grabbed her hand and gave it a squeeze. The principal went on to talk about what a great year it had been, but Casey wasn't listening. She was simply waiting for their names to be called up to the stage and then for her name to be announced as Prom Queen.

The principal finally called up the nominees. After announcing Casey and Robbie, the crowd applauded and cheered. Next, the principal called up Celeste and Brian and Casey swore the crowd seemed to cheer just a little louder for them. A wave of anger threatened to ruin this moment for Casey, but she swallowed it down. She waited patiently, gripping Robbie's arm as if it was a life raft.

"And now, it's finally time! This year's Prom King and Prom Queen goes to... Brian Parker and Celeste Matthews!!"

Casey's jaw dropped, stunned. The crowd erupted into cheers and applause. All eyes turned towards Celeste. Casey's breath hitched; she couldn't seem to catch it. Had the principal really just called Celeste's name instead of hers? This was her worst nightmare. A deep sadness overcame her, quickly followed by intense rage. Suddenly, a pounding started behind her eyes and just as she glimpsed her crown being placed atop Celeste's beautifully coiffed hair, she ran. Down the stage steps and out the entrance. Robbie quickly followed her, while the rest of the school cheered and clapped for their new Prom Queen, behind them.

"Casey, wait!" He yelled to her as she jogged over to his car. She was already yanking on the door handle, but it was locked. Robbie yelled again as he got closer, but it was like she couldn't even hear him. As he walked up and placed his hand on her shoulder, she spun around to face him. Robbie gasped and took a step back. Her face was bright red, but that wasn't what had frightened Rob. It was Casey's eyes. They looked black in the shadows of the streetlamps, and he could see the hatred in t hem.

Robbie shook off the dread he was feeling and unlocked the car doors. Without saying a word, Casey got in the passenger seat and Robbie jumped in the other side. He was nervous, he knew Casey took winning prom queen very seriously. He knew she also had some trouble controlling her emotions. But he had never seen her this angry before.

As he sat in the driver's seat and shut the door, he looked over at Casey. "You wanna just leave? We can, I don't mind."

She sat quietly without speaking for a moment and then answered, "What do you mean? They haven't announced the prom queen yet. I still need to get my crown, silly." Casey replied.

"Um, Cass. I'm sorry, but Celeste won. You know this," Robbie spoke softly.

"What do you mean? You want Celeste to be your queen?" Casey asked, her anger growing to a boiling point. She suddenly felt like Robbie was a stranger to her, maybe even secretly seeing Celeste behind her back. She snapped her head to the side and glared at him, trying to read his thoughts. All boys were the same. She was never enough. No, she didn't need a prom king. She would be the queen all by herself. She didn't need anyone, just her crown and the cheering crowd.

"I'm going to get my crown," she said to Robbie. She reached slowly up between her legs, causing Rob to exhale and smile, believing maybe she wanted to get frisky in the car. His smile was quickly wiped away as he saw Casey's arm flash in front of his face. Something silver glinted in the moonlight. Then he felt the pain and warmth ran down his chest.

He grabbed at his throat, still in disbelief, and felt the warm liquid. Casey watched, taking pleasure in his shock. She took her knife everywhere she went. You just never knew when you'd need it. She even ordered one of those thigh sheaths so she could bring it with her tonight. And now she was happy she did. Robbie had betrayed her, thinking Celeste deserved her crown. Well, she'd shown him.

Robbie continued to bleed out, slowly choking on his own vital fluid until finally slumping over his steering wheel. Casey didn't care about that, though; she was checking her makeup in the rearview mirror. She had to go get her crown, and she wanted to look her best.

As she got out of the car and walked back to the entrance, she noticed some dark spots on her dress. She knew immediately it was Robbie's blood, but luckily, she'd worn red, so it wasn't very noticeable. She knew tonight would be perfect. She smiled as she made her way through the door. Brianna almost walked directly into her.

"There you are! Oh my God, are you okay? I'm so sorry, Casey, I really thought you had this," Brianna said as she linked Casey's arm in her own.

"Everything is going to be perfect. I'm going to freshen up in the bathroom. Can you please send Celeste in? I just want to congratulate her." Casey replied with the biggest smile on her face. Brianna suddenly felt afraid of her friend. The look in her eyes gave Brianna a chill down her spine. She knew her friend had some pretty serious mental health problems, but Brianna had never seen it herself. Now she was questioning just how well she really did know her friend.

"Uh, yeah. Sure, of course. I'll let her know." Brianna answered and swiftly walked away. Casey looked around the dance floor. Her classmates' faces were all distorted now. They seemed to be laughing at her. But she was sure they would all go back to normal once she placed her crown on her head. Everything would be right then. So, she just smiled and continued towards the restrooms.

As she stood alone in the girls' bathroom staring at herself in the mirror, she watched as her face changed from beautiful to ghastly and then back to beautiful. For a split second, a rational voice spoke up in her mind, screaming at her, asking her what the hell she was doing. Casey quickly shoved that voice down and then ignored it. This was her night. Nothing would mess it up. She heard the creak of the bathroom door swinging open. Celeste stood there for a moment, Casey's crown atop her head.

"Hey, Casey. I'm so sorry you didn't win. Brianna said you wanted to talk to me?" Celeste spoke as she made her way into the large sink area.

Casey smiled her most friendly smile and walked past her to the door. She clicked the lock closed.

"Oh yes, Celeste, I do need to talk to you. You see, there's been a terrible mistake. I'm actually the Prom Queen, not you. So, if you want to just hand me my crown, everything will be right again." Casey slowly circled Celeste, like a wolf circling their prey.

"Uh, I don't think so, Casey. If there was a mistake, I'm sure Mrs. Hibbert would have told us. I'm really sorry you didn't win, though." Celeste told her, the kindness in her voice irking Casey.

"No. You're wrong. I did win. That's my crown, Celeste. And I'll just have to take it." Casey fiercely swung her fist into Celeste's face, causing her to crumble to the ground.

Before she had a chance to shake off the daze, Casey pounced and straddled her, locking Celeste's arms under her knees. She quickly covered Celeste's mouth with her left hand. In her right, she held her knife, still covered in Robbie's blood. When Celeste saw the blade, her eyes widened immediately and her struggle increased. The fear in those eyes gave Casey a comforting chill. Celeste didn't stand a chance.

Casey stabbed the knife down as hard as she could into the center of Celeste's throat. The blood spurted out and splashed Casey in her face. She laughed and slowly began sawing her knife back and forth.

Just as their peers began questioning where their prom queen and the runner-up were, Casey unlocked the bathroom door. She slowly pulled it open with one hand, while holding something heavy with her other. As the teens closest to her looked over, she heard loud gasps and even a scream. She knew she must look amazing, the most beautiful she'd ever looked.

The crowd continued to react to her as she walked towards the front of the hall. They parted, making a pathway for her, as she continued to the stage. None of the adults or teachers seemed to have spotted her yet. Casey climbed the steps, causing the DJ to stop the music and rush away from her. She grabbed the mic and stood at the front of the stage, looking down at her classmates.

That's when the screams really started, and more gasps of shock. Casey stood tall and confident. Her red dress was now soaked with blood, making it look almost black. Her crimson face dripped with gore. But that wasn't the only thing causing her peers to scream. In her left fist, she gripped Celeste's hair. The decapitated head swung back and forth slightly, the crown still sitting atop the severed head. Blood and viscera continued to drip from the gaping neck wound.

Casey picked up the mic and loudly exclaimed, "And now the time has come. Time to crown your Prom Queen!"

After placing the mic back down, Casey very carefully took the crown from Celeste's bloody head, the blonde hair now a deep crimson with blood. After securing the crown in her hand, she dropped Celeste's head as if it were no more than a piece of trash.

This was it, her moment. She could hear nothing now; all was silent in her mind. The screaming drowned out, the students running away, and some teachers rushing forward. None of it mattered. The only thing that mattered now was her finally becoming Prom Queen. Casey stood tall and confident as she placed the gleaming crown on her own head. Just as the distant sirens became clear, Casey smiled and said, "Casey Stiles, I now announce you Prom Queen."

6

— · —

The Glorious Adventure of The Premiere Size Queen of The Appalachian Trail Inside a Positively Gargantuan Cunt

By Anton Cancre

Dear Backpacker International Editorial Staff,

First timer, short timer here. I never, for a moment, would have thought it would happen to me. I hoped. Don't get me wrong there. Oh, gods of above, below, and sideways, did I hope for it. I just never expected it to actually happen. I mean, who the hell expects to end up full body down to the damn calves inside the silkiest fucking pussy they've ever come across or had come across them?

I feel like I need to back up a bit, though. Set the scene, if you will. Give a little context.

I was hiking the Appalachian trail. I can't say it was an accident, either. It all came from your own magazine. Sure, I was disappointed in the rag at first. Not at all what I expected or hoped for, to be honest. Reviews of hiking gear and talks with people who spend months out on trails. In retrospect, it makes sense. I've spent so long in my specific circle of interests that the possibility didn't even consider the merest chance of beginning to think about crossing my mind of there being a different meaning of "backpacking" outside of finding some tall, buff 'n burly Xena to throw you on her back and carry you around.

I'd spent fifteen bucks, though. Which is a tad steep per copy, by the way. I know you have to pay your writers and I appreciate articles written by actual human beings and all, but in a closed room, I am sure you would admit that's overboard. Anyway, I'd be damned if I wasn't gonna read it anyway after dropping that cash. And ya'll gave me some ideas.

Of course I heard of her. Poor lady just wouldn't stop growing. All manner of scientists and doctors trying their asses off to figure out why. Pollution runnoff. Steroids in the meat. Radiation. Fucking alien impregnation. Just your everyday average freak of nature situation. Whatever the hell caused it, we had an honest to goodness two and a half story tall woman out and proud in the world. Makes my forehead sweat just thinking about it now. Even if that is about all the sweating I can do anymore.

Big women always did it for me. I know, fucking cliche. Small dude like me, just on the edge of full out little person status, being into statuesque amazonian goddesses. Cliches exist for a reason, I guess. But I got this mailer once, back in the old days when places actually sent catalogs to your house. Not sure if a friend put me on a mailing list as a joke or my purchase history pointed a clear arrow at me, but this damn thing was full of the most outlandish porn you could think of in the cold pre-broadband internet days. All your usual barnyard and septic needs were represented on the cover, but it got so much weirder and intense inside. I was only twenty. An innocent babe unaware of many of my own inclinations, let alone the heights of depravity in others.

So, when I saw an ad for a video centered on one image, a woman with a man's head completely inside of her, I was struck. I laughed about it at first. Showed it to my friends. Did the whole "Isn't this weird and gross?" thing with them. But I kept going back to it. Eventually buying the video. VHS. That was how long ago this was. Wore the tape thin. Just about wore the skin on my dick clean through, too.

Fairly quickly, I was at the point where no one I could find or pay for could do the trick for me. Even when I finally found someone supple enough and willing to work with me. That wetness. that heat. That pressure. Wrapped around me.

It wasn't enough. There is only so much depth available, even with surgical alterations and medical abnormalities. At best, getting up to my chin. Whisps of wiry hair tickling my bare neck. Exciting. Intoxicating in its own way. Enough to get off, but not *enough*. Never *enough*. Not in the way I needed it to be.

Until I start hearing about her. Start seeing her on the Jerry Seinfeld and Maurice Popovitz shows. The only places a proper sideshow existed in America at the time. Now, even those are gone. Makes you weep for a lost time, ya know? Not saying that gawking at the weirdos is a good thing, but at least they weren't being swept under the carpet by people that still refuse to treat them like people even as they talk about how important acceptance is. Fucking hypocrite assholes.

Denise.

An unassuming name for the one who would become the center of my existence. One interview, she broke down, and they cut the feed. Not because she was crying. That shit is always ratings gold. Get you a fucking Emmy for your honesty and heartfelt portrayal and shit. No, they cut the feed because she was crying about not being able to catch a decent fuck. What is more human than that? Being horny. Being frustrated. Being absolutely crushed inside because you can't absolutely crush someone without literally crushing them. Knowing that even the most outsized freak of a polehauler can't do shit for you.

I can attest that love is great. Love is wondrous. Love can build and destroy empires. And love can't do shit against biological necessity.

I knew I didn't have love on offer any more than a proportionate cock. Hell, mine isn't even proportionate for my own diminutive size. But I could offer all of myself, in the most literal sense.

Denise went missing from the tabloids and trash TV and there was the same fucking war going on that had been there for the past 20 years as well as a couple new ones brewing and the latest vehement anti-gay senator had been caught chaining sixteen-year-old twinks up in their basement with a pound of butter and a gimp suit. Public attention had gone elsewhere, and it was clear that she wanted her own space. Wanted to be left alone.

That's when I remembered your spread on the Appalachian trail. Miles on miles of dense forest and nooks hidden among towering mountains. It was naïve to think I was the one to find her place. It was stupid to act like that was the only spot like it. It was, miraculously, kinda right.

Arrogant and idiotic. Shortsighted and simpleminded. Quitting my damn job. Cutting out on my lease. Selling my meager shit that would sell and throwing the rest in a dumpster behind Meijer. Then loading up on high protein and carbohydrate meals. Mostly in bar and tubed form because that is apparently the optimal calorie delivery system. Bought that OutdoorKwest 9000 pack you gave 5 stars to and a compressed, ultralight REI Trailface sack to sleep in. Then I hit the AT at the starting point in Springer Mountain and just went north.

Took a damn piece, too. No idea where to look, so just trekking the whole damn thing. One hundred percent certain that I wouldn't find her. But bound up in dreams all the same. Those dreams kept me together through both Carolinas and most of Virginia. They tightened my abs and locked my joints when I planked on the sheerest points of rock I could find. Play stiff as a board with myself, as it were. Wouldn't do any good to meet her and go all limp in my dear Denise's grasp, would it?

Was in Shenandoah that I heard her. A soft, deep moaning in the wind. Near midnight but I wanted to see Dark Hallow falls by moonlight. No mistaking that particular sound as the wind or a bear or some other numbskull nonsense. Undulating registers that moved the stone as much as the leaves. Not sure how long I pushed myself along, forcing through every bit of adrenaline left in me down that steep ass descent in the deep dark that only exists in a forest in the middle of the night.

Denise wasn't the first thing I saw. No. That was one of the others. Someone else with the same bright fucking idea as my own. Limp. Pallid grey despite what had likely been a deep sandalwood skin tone. Cock still impressively erect. A deep sense of satisfaction spread across his placid face.

Four inches doesn't sound like much. So, when I say that I saw her big toe, four inches from the middle knuckle down, pale and gleaming in the moonlight, digging into the dark Virginian soil, then you might be inclined to think that six inches isn't that much. Damn near as wide as it was long. It took me back. Those squirming piggies next to it. Grasping dirt and rock. Pulsing with moaning that had overcome the wind. Let me tell ya, son, that was a sight to behold.

That isn't getting into the arch leading up from them. The curve of ankle into calf and darkly fuzzed shin leading up the mountain. Yes, my girl's hairy. You think Gillette makes a Venus in actual goddess proportions? Besides, we're mammals, fucker. We come with hair. If that puts you off, go fuck a gecko. Personally, I had a hard time keeping myself from cumming on the spot.

My two hundred and fifty thousand lumen LED flashlight traced its way along the perfect bulge of her knee and up the impeccable meat of her thigh to the thickly furred cleft at her center. Soft, deep brown hair parting at the behest of fingers rubbing and thrusting with a gentle intensity.

Enraptured with the sight, I gasped. Held my breath as a sigh heaved down from the mountain and a loose form slid out from between the fingers, riding the moss-slicked stones down the falls. Her face beatific. A short, pixie-ish cut gone ragged and wild around her head. Glazed eyes staring content at the sky amid jutting, angular and misused bones that pointed in strange, unnatural directions. Was I jealous of her? She and several others I saw strewn amid the stones beneath the nethers of my dear needed Denise?

It would be a lie to say I wasn't. To say that I didn't want to be the one who realized her need and sought to fill it, alone. To say that I had not dreamed of being the only one to fill her and be the expression of her needs in base earthbound form. To leave her dreaming of me as I had dreamt of her, unknowing, for decades. I'm not an idiot.

That's the problem of being a dude, though, isn't it? You are told your whole life that you should be the one to wreck her shit like it's never been wrecked before. Don't just give her a good night. Don't just make her feel wanted or desired or fucking hot. Make her fucking cum like the world has never experienced before. Because YOUR dick is so goddamn amazing. If not, then you are just a little bitchboy in a sea of bitchboys.

Even knowing that, at the heart of it all, what I wanted was just for me. I read enough Freud to think of my own return to the womb in my cozy fantasies. If I wanted to provide for others, I could've learned how. Spent time on the proper tongue technique. Listened to the women I knew didn't want to fuck me, but bitched about the shit techniques of the dudes they did fuck. Dug beneath it for the truth of what they actually wanted. There was a reason I didn't have the time for that, and the reason was that I didn't fucking care.

So, seeing these bodies lying at odd angles along the sharp edges of the stones, bent by gravity and her muscular contortions, left me feeling jealous. Angry, to an extent. Hurt by a large margin.

All the same, I wasn't quite so blinded by my own self-importance to shuffle aside my desires. I won't say that I didn't take the time to think about how these bodies, coated in my most vaunted Denise's interior lubrication, brought her more or less pleasure than my own form could. I just realized that if I played my part to the hilt, then we could both get what we wanted from this.

Not too bad of a deal, all considered.

I won't lie and overblow my confidence in the moment. Walking up on a woman more than five times your own size is intimidating. Even mid clit rub with the still twitching and occasionally cold bodies of momentary lovers cast to the waters around you. Those waters running with as much cold blood and effluence as cum. Even with all the porns and shitty magazines of my youth screaming that a moment like this is a slam dunk, my nerves stabbed me right in the gut.

Unthinking, I stepped forward. At several points, someone lay in my path. This one's breath hitching with blood-clogged lungs. The next one shitting out their own entrails in thick blue ropes. Another a mess of mangled, misplaced limbs snapped and twisted into each other. There was no need to pay them any mind. I would suffer their fates and more just to feel her interior embrace. I'd made my choice.

Near enough and her musk was overpowering. Thick. Animalistic. Oily and somehow sweet. Intoxicating. Overwhelming. Just, well...

Fuck. I'm at a bit of a loss for words to describe it adequately. Just try, if you can, to remember the first time you found yourself face deep in someone's pussy. Not all Summer's Eve hospital disinfectant reek but the real shit. Skin and sweat and day long soaked in musk with the sheen of vaginal mucus all slick and sticky on your tongue and filling your nostrils. Meaty, but not in the food way.

Fleshy.

Yup. That's the word I'm looking for. Not something to fill you, but something to fill. Not a damn thing below the neck works on me, but I can sure as hell get my brain harder than a ten-peckered owl remembering that scent.

That's where I was. Standing between thighs pulled up toward her chest, thicker than any living tree trunks near us. Those fingers working lazy circles around a nub of flesh damn near the size of my head. Inflamed red and poking out from between her spread vulva. It was like the bright light of heavenly grace, were I to believe in such things.

Mist covered her from just below, her ribs on up. That saddened me. I hoped, if I could look into her eyes so far above me, that I'd see the same kind of hunger and need I felt. I went ahead and imagined the face I saw so often on tv. Tawny and glowing like beach sand at sunset. Those soft brown eyes, pinched nose and sharp-angled chin. Thin, pink lips split with mischief just enough to reveal gleaming teeth that could well be my tombstone and I wouldn't care in the slightest. All framed by curls and waves of hair so deeply brown as to be almost black. A starlet from Hollywood's golden age so much larger than any silver screen could fit.

It was definitely do or die time. I stepped in closer.

I began caressing the edges of her vulva. The rough texture of her pubic hair maddened me. Every primal piece of me screamed to dive into her like the deep waters of a lagoon. I knew better than that. If there was time, there would be time. I was here and there was no need to rush it.

Maybe she moaned. I want to believe that was what I heard. Not the wind blowing low through the trees and mountains, but a catch of pleasure in her lungs. Her fingers stayed their course around and over her clit. I kept my hand in rhythm with them.

Her hips rolled, edging her towards me. A slight enough movement for her, but it damn near knocked me on my ass. My face pressed for the moment against her minora. I couldn't help myself but run my tongue along that velvety flesh to taste her. I can't remember the flavor. Can you imagine that bullshit? Too overcome by the electricity pulsing through me. The excitement that wracked my body with convulsions and the pulsing of my prostate in an unexpected and positively devastating orgasm. If I have any regrets, that's where they lay.

I wonder what it felt like for her. Probably nothing. Maybe the slightest wisp of a nerve lit up, like being brushed by the leg of an ant or kissed by the wing of a butterfly.

That's when I felt a grip on my legs and hip. Probably not the entirety of her hand. Enough of it to hold me firm, though. I took the cue and stiffened myself. Remembered my breathing and locked both joint and muscle. Tightening and loosening just the right ones to keep my body rigid. Even when she had me in dead, open air, I was stone made flesh. Rigid and strong.

Now, any free diver will tell you that you think you can hold your breath until you are 200 meters down and your lungs are screaming for air but you still have that same amount back to the surface and have to ignore every natural impulse at one third of the way to open your mouth and suck in whatever is around you before the blackness takes you in. I'd followed tutorials online. Swum out into open ocean and straight down. Practiced timing myself in my fucking bathtub. Not a damn bit of that prepared me for being down past my hips in muscles that squeezed to just the point of collapse before releasing. Pulling you back out into open air for the merest second of a chance to gulp in a breath before slamming you back in. A nail of what I presume was the other hand scraping raw skin from your back at periodic, random intervals.

It was everything I'd hoped for. Everything I'd dreamt of. But so much more than I'd understood. The in-out in-in-in-in-out-in-in of it all. I remember my collar bones breaking. My knees cracking and twisting the wrong direction. My spine. Something happened. Something like the wondrous, snap-crackle-pop of existence. I was born and unborn times beyond counting. Bones kneaded. Organs rearranged. Skullmeat compressed to a single searing point of incandescence. Physical, psychological, spiritual, and philosophical upheaval via pressure and release.

I heard and felt undulations undreamt of. I knew her pleasure through her flesh. I filled a need left empty by eyes that desired and despised in equal measure. I, among so many others, helped her feel human for a screaming into the uncaring sky ecstasy moment. We helped her cast aside the stares and the judgment and the assumption that existence must be in one singular manifestation.

Explosions of light and color. The dense interiority of experience occurred. I don't know what the fuck you want from me here. I wasn't, and I was. I am now and will never have been. My experience of Denise and her experience of me were. I still am. I'm not sure why. I assume someone else saw me. Did what they could to preserve flesh and neural connection to it. They wanted to help, and I can't blame them for it.

How could they know the ecstasy? How can they comprehend, never having experienced, a moment wherein all later moments cease to bear importance? How could I convey to them, even with the few words that remain to me, how complete I am now?

I've begged them to stop hunting her already. I don't know what good it will do, knowing the hate held by those that can't find what they desire. What anger the weakened harbor toward those with strength they didn't ask for. But I've done my best to try to not to be another excuse of violence as a response to inadequacy and erectile dysfunction. I hope

Denise is still out there and that they haven't turned her into another example of what happens when the vaginally enhanced make the mistake of acting in their own interest for once.

I hope that those who found me crushed and content did not take my lack of vocal capability as encouragement of their rage. Of support for their assault on someone who possesses what they lack. Of some resentment based on what I now lack in comparison to the experience that lead me to this state, have not pushed further against those who did not choose their present state and still refuse to find shame in it. I hope that my dearest Denise, who had the presence of mind to flee the scene where my own shattered form was found, has found her own peace somewhere in the world and is not lying, broken and rotting along some abandoned riverside. All of us forgotten and grotesque beings deserve our futures, dearest.

Anyway, I wanted to thank you for all you do. If you ever think about shutting down, please remember that there is a quadriplegic out there who would never have gotten nearly his entire body shoved into a giant's pussy repeatedly until the vast majority of his bones were crushed and nerves rendered useless were it not for the work of your fine writing staff. It has meant the world to me.

Thankfully and gratefully,
Ben Gifford

7

The Toxins

By Kenzie Jennings

"Have you ever considered stabbing someone in the face?"

Martin was on a roll, his bloodshot eyes darting this way and that as he waved around the butcher knife he'd brought into the office that day. He poked the air in front of Dana, his supervisor at the dealership, the tip of it jabbing between her eyes.

"Like that," he said, prodding the air, the tip of the blade mere inches away from her pallid face.

Some of Martin's colleagues on staff that day were watching from their desks. Others gaped from the café counter with its coffee maker and ever-changing boxes of stale donuts from the donut shop next door to the dealership. A few coworkers were even sneakily filming the action happening right outside Dana's office.

Everyone was dying to see this go down. No one, however, expected Martin to be the one doing the confronting. He was normally the nicest, most well-adjusted salesman on the floor.

Something had to give though, and Dana would bear the brunt

"Martin, please put the knife away," Dana said as calmly as she could muster, given the circumstances. "We can chat like rational human beings, okay? You'd mentioned we'd neglected your overtime? We can work that out with payroll. I'm sure it was just an oversight on their part. Maybe Marsha can—"

"Shut the FUCK UP!" Martin's face had gone a deep shade of violet, his spittle flying from the corners of his mouth. "You have NO idea what it's like to be in my shoes, so don't act like you're the queen of empathy, you uppity fuck. I swear, if I have to hear another pathetic story about your Ivy League, stick-up-his-ass grandson...or what stupid asshole thing your husband did on some outdated piece of technology...Newsflash, Dana, no one has a fucking flip phone anymore!"

By then, the police had arrived, and two burly uniforms had flanked Dana, ready to take Martin down, but Martin held firm, his grin taking control.

"I've learned a lot in the past couple of months, you know," he continued, turning the knife in his grip, "and I realized that the only way you can get rid of the people on your back...and the voices in your head...is to do it good and hard to yourself, like this..."

That, right there, was the moment he stabbed himself in the face. Granted, it wasn't a killing blow, of course, but judging by the way he'd yanked out the knife from his cheek and continued to stab himself again...and then again...one could surmise the entire point he wanted to make was one of a slow, painful, *memorable* ending.

By the time he'd finished, it was the stockier of the policemen who'd ended it right after Martin had driven the blade into an artery and then ripped.

It had been a good, productive day.

"THERE IS *NOTHING* LIKE the first bite of a fresh navel orange before breakfast. You know that sensation of the tart, succulent bite bursting between your teeth, right? But it's gotta be good. It's gotta be fresh..."

She was beautiful, that Buffie LaRoux. Mesmerizing, magnetic, all of it.

Heather set her cell in its stand on the kitchen counter while she diced herbs for the pasta dish she was diligently making.

Not like she *had* to do it.

Except that *she* had to do it.

"Babe, how much longer? I'm getting hangry here," Jayce called out from the living room.

"I dunno. Maybe twenty minutes?"

Jayce let out a loud sigh that echoed throughout their tiny apartment. The guy was the king of exaggerated pauses and melodramatic grunts. "I haven't had anything to eat since earlier today. It's been hours," he whined. "I'm starving."

"What the hell, Jayce? I packed you lunch. What, you eat it early or something?"

"Well, I had to. You didn't have breakfast ready for my shift."

Heather halted her chopping and stared hard at the knife in her grip. It would be so easy to slice open his throat, probably even satisfying. She imagined the blade sliding, digging into the soft flesh, tearing the meat wide open.

The oven timer went off, breaking Heather away from her intrusive thoughts. The garlic loaf was ready, its pungent aroma wafting through the kitchen. Heather set down the knife and put on the oven mitts, shoddy things from Jayce's mother printed with cutesy farm animals. Jayce's mother often treated them both as if they were thirty years younger, and Heather couldn't stand it, especially since she had to live with a guy who'd been so spoiled throughout his childhood into his adult life. Jayce's mom would blatantly hint at Heather as to what sort of role her lazy son's girlfriend was "supposed to" take on, the same sort of role Jayce's mom had clearly been acclimated to for decades.

"Smells so good, babe!"

Buffie LaRoux's sunkissed Malibu Barbie face filled the cell frame, her smile warm and inviting. "That first bite of the orange is your first taste of what it feels like to get rid of those toxins, all those poisons inside and out..."

"Hey, babe, just so you know, I was going to set the table," Jayce prattled, "but you already did it, and you do a much better job, anyway."

From a kitchen knife to a scalding tray of garlic bread, the weapons were all right there, ready for *good* use. Heather set the tray down on the other end of the counter, deep in her own head, as ever, but Buffie LaRoux—Queen Buffie LaRoux of her Toxicologie kingdom—soothed the monster lurking there in Heather with her sugary tones and smile full of California sunshine.

"Only $34.95 to begin your experience with me. Become a Toxinator with membership dues of $15.95 per month for unlimited access to Toxicologie and its participating partners, with up to sixty percent off all our products, including our newest addition to our spa and wellness line, our Goddess Gua Sha set—"

"Did she seriously just say 'Toxinator'?"

Heather jumped at the sound of Jayce's voice directly behind her. The bread knife she'd pulled out of the knife holder slipped from her grip and clattered on the floor. Jayce chortled at Heather's clumsiness, and he wrapped his arms around her, one hand squeezing a breast, the other stroking her belly.

He nuzzled her ear, murmuring, "All those carbs. What say we work it off later on? I'll eat you out like I did the other night. We could even sixty-nine it. Remember when we used to do that? It's been awhile..."

There was a reason it had been a while, but Heather wasn't about to get into it. The last time she'd tried to direct Jayce to the right spots, the ones directly in front of his eyes, he'd grown all sensitive and huffy, insisting he knew "exactly" what he was doing.

"...Isn't it time to take control of *your* lifestyle?" Buffie LaRoux continued, her tone having gone much more overt and sharp. "So, what are you waiting for? Toxins out, energy in all the way..."

"Isn't that what your liver's for?" Jayce said, a smirk in his tone. "Didn't she take a biology class?"

Heather didn't care for his tenor. That holier-than-thou, depreciating smugness, like he was more knowledgeable than anyone else. "Toxicologie has ample peer reviewed research behind many of their products, including the protein packs they sell. It's a lifestyle brand, that's all."

"It's a cult, babe." Jayce let go of Heather's waist just to reach around her and tear off a hunk of garlic bread, which he then shoved into his maw and chewed noisily. "An' you don't wanna be in a cult, do you?" he said around the wet, doughy mush, bits of bread spitting from his mouth. "We gonna eat now or what?"

He grinned, and all Heather wanted to do was get the kitchen knife and scrape the sticky wads of dough from between his teeth...

...right before she carved out his tongue.

⬤

"HAVE YOU TRIED THE beetroot shot? Sam told me it made her dizzy for a day or two, but a couple days in, and she felt like she'd orgasmed all afternoon." Mel, one of Heather's close friends from the office, had taken a long slug of her SuperQueen SuperGreen Smoothie right before she'd told Heather all about the miracle of a Toxicologie beetroot shot.

They'd been at lunch for barely ten minutes in the breakroom before Mel had gone into full Toxicologie mode.

Like a good little cult member, babe.

Richie from sales plopped down in the empty chair beside Mel. He was wearing the lavender button-down, which meant he and his partner had made up from their last row. Heather loved that he color coded his outfits to match his mood. Unlike her other friends, there was no hidden pretense with Richie.

"Are we talking about the beetroot shot?" he said, unzipping his lunch bag. "I heard it makes you feel like you had a full body massage. Get you all relaxed and glowy, all those amazing ingredients." He made a face at Mel's smoothie. "And that *has* to be the SuperQueen smoothie. Someone said it has jellyfish in it. Is that true? Jellyfish? Does it taste like sea snot?"

Mel wrinkled her nose at him before she took another swig. She then smacked her lips in his face. "Tastes more like tart green apples and the kiss-my-ass tears of my enemies, darling."

Richie barked out a laugh. "Shit those bitter toxins right out."

"Say when," said Mel, grinning at him. "I'll cleanse myself out right at your feet all over those $700 shoes."

Heather enjoyed the banter, but she wasn't about to keep her curiosity at bay. Not when "toxins" were the problems of the month. "Didn't *you* get on the Toxicologie train, Rich?"

"Girl, I been riding all the way to clean town since May. Have you seen my skin lately?" Richie stuck his neck out, turning his head this way and that for both Heather and Mel to notice. "Look at that glow there. Baby fresh skin. Baby fresh."

"How many babies did you have to ingest to get it there?" Mel said with a grimace.

"One in every shade, bitch. Pop them in a blender with some kelp gravy and apple cider vinegar. Delicious."

"God, you two are disgusting." Heather took out her Thermos and poured some soup from it into the lid cup as Mel and Richie continued their grotesque banter.

They're in deep, babe. Real deep.

It was Mel who drew away first, her attention diverted towards Heather's cup of soup. "You should try it out," she said to Heather. "I mean, we joke about it, sure, but let me tell you, I've *never* felt this good since I got onboard. It's like a weight has lifted not just off me, but *out* of me...out of my whole system. It's even improved Richie's relationship. It's that good."

Heather swiveled in Richie's direction. "Really? How so?"

Richie shrugged. "Martin found nirvana. I found peace and quiet."

Heather's eyes widened at the thought.

"What can I say, girl? It works," he said with a grin.

———◆○◆———

"Now that you've completed the first step of your journey, you're on your way to becoming a true Toxinator."

Heather giggled into her hand. Jayce had had a point. The terminology, the lingo, was ridiculous. Still, she wasn't about to give up, especially since she'd dropped several hundred dollars on the Toxin Eliminator III package that consisted of her first box of "groceries" and full access to the website.

Heather removed one of her earbuds as she sat there in the dim light of her iPad, the only light illuminating the darkened curve of the bedroom. Jayce's deep snoring signaled to her that she was perfectly fine watching Buffie LaRoux's videos, one by one, in bed without worrying whether or not she'd woken him. Heather put her earbud in and settled back against the bedframe to watch the next video.

This time, Buffie LaRoux had specific instructions, a sexy assistant with washboard abs, and props.

Props that would prove not all that difficult to procure.

As soon as Heather completed the video, she shut off her iPad and set it on the nightstand. Then she scooted down deep underneath the duvet, pulled down Jayce's boxer briefs, and took him in her mouth.

———◆○◆———

"Full on Toxinator, girl," Richie said as he settled into a brisk walk on the treadmill next to Heather's at the gym. "What I like to see."

Heather drank the remnants of the smoothie she'd brought with her that she'd poured into her Toxicologie Travel Thermos, one of those insulated types that kept the drink hot or cold for hours on end.

One of the many perks one could enjoy upon joining Buffie LaRoux's Toxicologie army. Heather was intent on going through the entire program until she reached full Toxinator status, a coveted reward at the end being an all-expenses paid trip to Honolulu for Toxicolmania the following year.

"You'll feel the effects after a few days." Richie poked at the accelerator button until his treadmill was rolling at a faster pace that had him moving in a steady jog. "Believe me, it'll change everything from the inside...out," he said, panting at the sudden switch in pace. "That roll around your middle, gone, girl, GONE."

"I'm not doing it to lose weight," huffed Heather. "I'm perfectly happy with my physical health."

Richie let out a cackle, whole and spiky. "We go all in with our bodies in mind first. Who do you think you're fooling here, honey? It's a physical health journey Queen Buffie has us on, sacrificing all our blood, sweat, and tears."

"Was Martin a part of *your* 'physical health journey', then?"

Richie punched the off button and held onto the bar as his treadmill came to a stop. He then turned to Heather, who slowed her treadmill speed so that she could focus her attention on him.

"Martin didn't have anything to do with it," he said sharply. "It was *my* journey to help with *my* issues. Let me tell you something...Ain't no Queen Buffie, Muffie, Duffie, or Huffie LaRoux in *my* world, taking charge of what *I* need. I joined for *me.*"

"That's not what I—"

Richie held up a palm in her direction. "No. *You* don't get to make fun. You don't get to judge my choices, *my* decisions, and you sure as shit don't get to play Bitch Queen with a sassitude. You wanna play in the Toxicologie world? Well and good, but you gotta check yourself before you judge others. It's part of the Covenant."

"The what now?"

Richie let out an incredulous snort before deadpanning her once again. "You need to go back and actually read the agreement you signed before you paid for your membership. Maybe once you do, you'll have a better attitude about what you signed up for."

With that, Richie left her there to scroll through the Toxicologie homepage on her cell to find out what the "Covenant" was.

According to the Member Agreement, each rule in the Covenant had to be followed to the letter.

The thought of that alone sent a strange chill through Heather...

...and, frankly, it was pretty exciting.

"YOUR DEMEANOR REFLECTS THE brand." Buffie LaRoux's voice had taken a somber tone, breaking from her usual chipper self. "A negative attitude can affect your overall wellbeing, and the toxins will curdle. Your liver will hate you as much as you hate yourself. The only way to get out of that negative slump is to enact change."

"Ooooh, sounds like a mind-over-body matter," Jayce said from the kitchen.

Heather hadn't even realized just how loud the volume on her iPad was, so she turned it down to a whisper. She hated the thought of Jayce poking fun at her new venture into the world of health and wellness, her "cult" as Jayce had put it.

Something had to give though, and there had been something certainly *off* about the past couple of weeks.

One thing she hadn't seemed to notice until then was the fact that *Jayce was in the kitchen.*

He was cooking, actually *cooking.*

The guy hadn't ever touched a kitchen pan or an appliance for as long as she'd known him.

Suddenly, he taken an "interest"?

"You're gonna find that every single toxin that has been plaguing your world with bloat and bile, all those poisons, will be eliminated from your life completely," Buffie LaRoux continued, startling Heather out of her thoughts. "And as a Toxinator, you'll have the ability to pass on your knowledge to others like you who've been poisoned by dangerous ingestibles and society's expectations, everything that's killing the world, one disease, one virus, one *toxin*, at a time."

"Almost ready, babe! I'll set the table in a minute, so don't get up."

For once, Jayce wasn't his usual snarky self, which shook Heather even more. The aroma coming from the kitchen, a pungent blend of herbs and spices, was almost impossible to resist.

Curry, maybe?

But Jayce didn't like anything "exotic." He'd always been a steak and potatoes kind of guy. He'd complain every time Heather had attempted to introduce anything new to him.

Heather left Miss LaRoux and made her way from the den to the dining area of the living room. Sure enough, the table had been set with her own best china—the kind reserved for company. There were even meticulously folded linen napkins, and Heather hadn't even realized they'd *owned* linen napkins.

Jayce emerged from the kitchen carrying a Dutch oven between his mitts on each hand, taking Heather completely aback.

He was even wearing his best dress shirt and trousers, and he'd shaved the five o'clock shadow.

Heather suddenly felt dowdy having gotten into her lounge pajamas right after she'd come home from work, her settled routine that she swore she'd change for no one.

Jayce handed her a frosty glass of beer, his eyes sparkling in the candlelight.

(*Candlelight?*)

"I figured it would go well with chicken tikka masala. Got a nice bite to it," he said.

Heather took a tentative sip. It was cool and perfectly sour, going down smoothly.

"Thought you could use a break," he continued. I know how unhappy you've been, and I feel like it's been me."

"C'mon, Jayce..."

"No, let me finish. I don't deserve you, H. I wanna make this right."

"Step one in your journey," Buffie LaRoux's honey and lavender voice purred from the den, "*Acquiescence.*"

"Let's eat," said Jayce, holding out a hand to Heather so he could lead her to her chair at the table. "Your throne at the table awaits, madame. Later tonight, we'll make another one for you on my face."

And just like that, Jayce was back in character, much to Heather's relief...

...somewhat.

⸻◆⸻

"Step two," said Buffie LaRoux. "Antipathy."

"If you don't wanna eat your banana pudding, give it here. Don't let it go to waste." Richie held out his hand impatiently in Mel's direction. "I will die in a vat of that shit. I don't care if it's part of the Toxicologie Plan or not."

Mel slid the container across the table towards Richie. "It tastes like sour milk."

"How long have you had it?" Richie opened the container and sniffed its contents. "Doesn't smell bad."

"I stopped in Zeb's for my coffee this morning and saw they had a fresh batch out. Stuff's been my favorite since I was a kid."

"Girl, me too. I love this so much." Richie took out a spoon and blended the contents so that the whipped topping became one with the pudding. "Mama used to soak the bananas in rum. *So* good."

While Richie and Mel reminisced about banana pudding, Heather was taking her sweet time, enjoying the smoothie she'd brought, savoring the taste. She'd grown used to the slightly chlorinated aftertaste of Jayce's semen, which served to balance the bitterness of the greens and the sweetness of the agave.

"Do you feel guilty about this like I do?" Mel prodded. "I dunno. Every time I try to eat something off book, it's nasty. It's like my tastebuds are all screwed up."

"Think about how good you'll feel, though," Heather said. "If the only pleasure you get when you're eating is if you eat anything that's part of the Plan, that's a win for your health, isn't it?"

Mel shrugged. "Maybe, but I don't like what it's done to the foods I love. Doesn't the Plan have cheat days?"

By then, Richie had already dug right into the banana pudding, taking a big scoop and shoveling it into his mouth. As soon he tasted it, he winced and spat it out into his napkin. "That tastes like a mixture of vomit and ass dung."

'That's redundant," Heather said, chuckling.

Richie shot her a puzzled frown. "What is?"

"Ass dung? Where else does dung come from?"

Mel snickered, but quickly smothered it when Richie swiveled in her direction. "What, it tastes like shit, right? You can just say that."

"Anyway, if the Plan has affected our sense of taste," said Heather, "then how come I enjoyed the chicken tikka masala Jayce made for me last night?"

Mel focused on Heather, her eyes wide in happy surprise. "He cooked for you? He did not!"

"Bitch, you lie," Richie scoffed. "Ain't no way that boy stopped playing Fortnite or whateverthefuck to make you something to eat."

"*You* try it then." Mel took the container from Richie and set it in front of Heather. "Maybe it'll taste normal to you."

But it didn't. In fact, the pudding tasted like curdled milk...that topped a bit of ass dung. Heather rushed to the sink to spit it out and then rinse her mouth out under the faucet.

It wasn't until Carlie from Payroll trudged in to get her lunch from the refrigerator when Richie had an idea. Carlie was her usual delightful self with her face pinched in a permanent constipated expression that bunched further at Richie when he offered her the pudding.

"Why, what's in it?" she said.

"Girl, nothing. It's just banana pudding. Mel got it at Zeb's, so you know it's good."

"I'm allergic to nuts, just so you know."

Richie rolled his eyes, exasperated already. "Since when does banana pudding have nuts in it? Just try it," pressed Richie, holding out the container for Carlie.

Carlie took it tentatively and stirred the contents around before taking a bite.

Apparently, the pudding was as "delicious" as Mel had initially hoped.

"Well, damn," muttered Richie. "Our tastebuds really *are* screwed up."

"Can I have this? I promise I'll wash out the container." Carlie then took another big bite and another.

Mel waved it away. "By all means. Enjoy."

"Thanks." Just before Carlie left the trio to mull their unfortunate discovery, she turned back around. "Don't forget timesheets are due by three."

"You see her sweater?" said Richie after Carlie had left. "The iguanas all over? How much you wanna bet she's wearing the vest tomorrow, the one with the—"

"The squirrels? That one!" Mel snickered before she smothered her mouth once more, which sent the two of them into a snickering fit.

Heather, however, wasn't amused.

She realized, quite frankly, her world would likely be so much more peaceful without those two in it.

TEN MINUTES INTO THEIR lovemaking late that night, Jayce had Heather stop. She'd been enjoying the position, sitting with their legs interlocked, like a knotted puzzle. The friction had been delicious. Stopping though was distracting, and Heather didn't care for distractions, especially when Jayce had seemed more than willing to try something besides taking her from behind, his favorite pastime.

"What's wrong?"

He just sat there, staring blankly at her, not saying a word while still inside her.

It was as if he had been...

...switched *off*.

"Jayce?"

He didn't say anything. The only sounds in their bedroom were the clicking of the clock on the nightstand and Heather's panting from the workout they'd endured. Jayce, though, didn't seem to be breathing at all.

He then suddenly made an awful face at her, contorting his features, his nose crinkling. Jayce looked at Heather as if he'd found the remnants of a cockroach in his shoe, and she was the cockroach corpse.

That erection that had been something fierce, almost otherworldly so but in all the best possible ways, was nonexistent as he slid out of her.

Heather sat there, too stunned to properly react as Jayce moved off the bed and padded to their en suite bathroom without saying a word.

"What the hell, Jayce?" she said in the dark.

Even the dark wasn't interested anymore.

"The final step," Buffie LaRoux said into the lens. The camera had zoomed in on her beautiful features, focusing on her bright emerald eyes, eyes where the skin around them bore virtually no wrinkles, no telltale signs of Buffie LaRoux's possible age. "The point where everything changes for the better. The point when you realize you're free, and what better way to ensure your freedom that last, crucial step. Are you ready?" Those eyes smiled in the frame, coaxing the viewer to listen closely.

"Step three: Eradication. All those toxins, the ones remaining, clinging to your system like parasites, they'll be gone. Think about how free you'll be. Think about how lighter you'll feel. Your mind and body will thank you for it."

Jayce had cleared out all of his belongings from the apartment by the time Heather had come home from work. She would've been home much earlier if it hadn't been for the gridlock on the interstate due to an accident at the turnpike near the bridge. Their little abode felt bare without all the electronics and his hideous pieces of furniture, from the den desk down to his gaming chair.

Heather dropped her tote on the breakfast bar as she'd routinely done for the four years they'd lived there. She went from room to room, trying to find any hint of Jayce left, but even his hair gel and the pile of laundry on the closet floor were gone.

Fuck him, Heather thought. He'd grown into such a thorn, always poking and prodding her to do the bulk of the housework and every bit of the emotional labor.

Fuck. Him.

He could've said something, right? Isn't that what happens in a normal breakup?

Heather stuck to her routine, fuming as she got into her PJs and unclipped her hair, letting it go wild and free.

Jayce had always loved that part. Heather was convinced he'd been with her only for her hair.

Fuck. *Him.*

With a glass of cheap cabernet in hand, Heather settled down on the sectional sofa—a piece of furniture that had been the only one she and Jayce could agree on—and switched on the evening news.

"...body identified as Jayson Rhodes, a forty-six year-old resident of Deltona. Rhodes had apparently jumped from—"

Heather quickly shut off the TV, her heart thudding in her ears.

"Eradication. All those toxins," echoed Buffie LaRoux. *"Can you imagine that?"*

"Yes," whispered Heather. "Yes, I can."

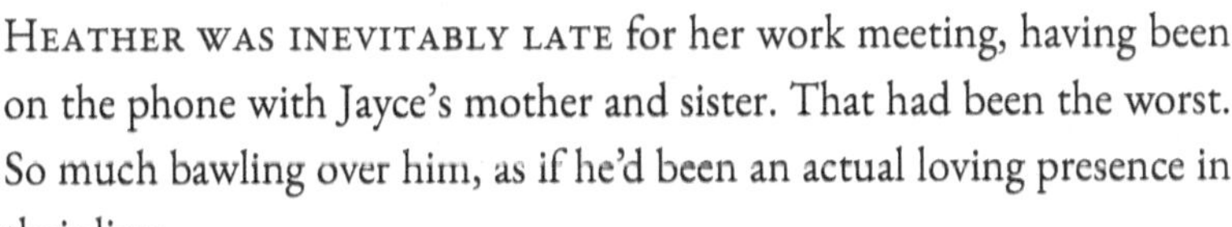

HEATHER WAS INEVITABLY LATE for her work meeting, having been on the phone with Jayce's mother and sister. That had been the worst. So much bawling over him, as if he'd been an actual loving presence in their lives.

Heather couldn't have cared less the more she thought about it.

Buffie LaRoux had been right.

She *was* free, but for some reason, the bloat was still a nagging presence in her gut, in her sides. Maybe an apple cider vinegar shot would help, followed by a ginger peach smoothie.

Yes, that sounded divine. That would do.

"Heather! So nice of you to finally join us." Marilyn, her boss who'd been conducting the presentation of the company's sales for the quarter, an incredibly longwinded meeting that could've easily been an email, stopped mid-sentence just as Heather had snuck in, sitting in a chair in the back row.

She winced at the call out and mouthed a "Sorry."

Richie and Mel were seated in the row directly in front of her. Mel leaned in, craning towards Heather. "Hey," she whispered, beckoning with her head for Heather to scoot closer. "Wanna know what it's like to slip rat poison into everyone's pastries and coffee?"

"Yeah, fuck their pastries," muttered Richie.

"What?" Heather couldn't move from her seat, couldn't budge at all. Her heart dropped. Her stomach went sour.

When Steve from HR, who'd been standing near Heather, threw up, splattering her in sticky blood, that was when she finally found the will to jolt out of her chair, gasping.

Ellen, Salesperson of the Quarter five years in a row, followed suit, keeling over as thick ropes of blood streamed out of her mouth, soaking the striped carpet.

By then, nearly every other colleague at the meeting had hit the floor, rolling out of their chairs, puking up whole clots and threads.

By then, it was absolute madness.

Mandy, Marilyn's assistant, was the first to die lying there, right to the other side of Heather. Her eyes had rolled back in her head after she'd convulsed, her chin and entire dress drenched in blood.

Heather was already eyeing the exit. Her path, however, held too many obstacles.

Carlie was trying her best to resuscitate Marilyn, who'd gone pasty grey, her own blood having doused the projection screen and computer at the podium.

The unaffected colleagues were either panicking, rushing out of the conference room, or attempting to aide others, following Carlie's lead.

Richie and Mel, on the other hand, gave each other a friendly air kiss before they both took out the pistols they'd evidently snuck in that morning somehow and promptly shot themselves in the head.

Heather found herself being ushered out of the room. Her mind by then was too far gone to determine how she'd actually managed to leave. Her body no longer felt like her own. Her legs took her places, but she simply couldn't react.

She was perfectly, almost serenely, numb all over.

The truth of the matter was that she felt pretty good.

In fact, she felt fucking fantastic.

Aside from the bit of bloat still around her waistline, it was amazing what a Toxicologie Detox Plan could do in a matter of weeks.

And Heather knew exactly what she had to do to *Eradicate* the last of those pesky toxins from her life.

She followed some of her colleagues up to the roof of their building, seventeen stories up.

One by one, they stepped off the ledge, plunging all the way down to the empty construction site in the back of their building, their bodies bursting and cracking against the ground, like skin balloons filled with blood, gristle, and bone.

As for Heather, she dove head first.

If anything, to get rid of that last bit of bloat, that last toxin—

Herself.

8

— · —

No Shelter Here

By Michael R. Collins

Willow Estes shivered against the chill night. She hadn't planned on walking so far tonight, and her ratty black hoodie was not up to the task. The sudden cold spell caught her off guard. Truth be told, the entire night caught her off guard. The weight of her black backpack drooped her shoulders. As did the weight of her life. All she wanted to do was get out of the cold for a few minutes and get something to eat. It was her first night back in her hometown and it already had become a nightmare. Her hands shook as she wiped the red speckles on her jeans.

Few cars were out at this time of night. All the businesses were dark and locked against her, even for a moment's respite from the icy breezes. Modern construction was specifically designed to give no shelter for people who lived on the street. She'd only been homeless for a couple months, but it didn't take long to learn how invisible a person could be. And how discarded.

Loss of job, loss of housing, and loss of friends when the going got tough, and what little family she had left spread too far out, all contributed to her living on the streets. Coming back here was not her plan, but it was as far as she could get. Willow hoped to get a couple more hours down the road, but this was as far as her ride was going. She had little love for this town, and less so for the people who still lived here. And now she was on the run.

Desperation subsided enough for her to think clearly. She remembered a diner being nearby. If she could make it there, everything would be alright. At least for the moment.

Looking up from her battered canvas shoes, a light blazed, reflecting off the glass and chrome. A tall sign in the corner of the parking lot shone as a bright beacon to all who might want to visit the Queen City Diner. A thin haze hung around it, extending into the street. Willow pulled the hood down over her eyes as a car sped past her. For the hundredth time, she rubbed her hands against her pants before jamming them back into her pockets. The few dollars and loose change should be enough for coffee and food.

Her feet hurt from walking, and her fingers ached from the cold. Nothing about this night had gone right, which was par for the course. She'd be the first to admit. Coming back to town was a mistake. Those who could not be trusted remained consistent.

The bright lights hurt as she gripped the chrome door handle and pulled. A bell jingled above. The warm smell of coffee, pancakes, and seared hamburger caressed her nose. It was just as she remembered. Childhood memories danced around the edges of her mind.

"Welcome to Queen City Diner. Just one? Follow me." A waitress told her from behind the small counter near the door. She was young and peppy, her face painted with optimism. Her quick smile made Willow relax, but only in small increments. She knew the girl was vying for good tips. Willow waitressed for a short time before landing on the streets. No one enjoyed working in diners. It was always somewhere you wound up.

"Thanks," she mumbled as she was led to a back booth by one of the large windows. She scanned the room, checking the other patrons. There weren't many. Two seats ahead of her, an old man sipped noisily at the soup of the day. His hand slowly dipped the spoon in the cloudy broth, then, just as slowly, brought it to his lips. He didn't care how loud or long he slurped each spoonful.

Near the front sat a mother and child, both murmuring to each other. The boy couldn't have been more than four years old. The mother, with her fire-engine-red hair, leaned in to conspire with the child. *Seems a little late to feed little Timmy pancakes and chocolate milk*, Willow thought, *but who am I to say?* The child looked at her, judging her at a much more advanced age than most toddlers.

Beside her was a young couple. The two male teens tittered and touched each other's hands as they waited for their orders. If Willow had any love in her heart tonight, she'd find it cute. They were oblivious to everything around them, as if the world ceased to exist beyond the sphere of their adorations.

An old woman glowered a few seats ahead of the lovers. She glared at them with vicious intensity, taking small breaks to glare at everybody else. Her gaze landed on Willow, and she blinked. The woman's lids blinked sideways. Willow looked away, blaming stress and fatigue for making her eyes play tricks on her.

At the counter a man stooped over, his back to her. His puffy black coat hid his frame, and a black hood covered his head. He picked at a gooey slice of apple pie, a scoop of ice cream lazily melting next to it.

The perky young waitress worked alongside an older woman. The older woman's movements were slow and exhausted. In the kitchen, a beefy cook sweated over the griddle. He squinted in anger at the food he cooked.

"Maybe this wasn't a good idea," Willow whispered. Could they tell what she had done? Would they sneak off to call the police? She peered out the dark window. No one was out there, not even late-night traffic anymore. Best to stay put. She eyed the man at the counter. Something about him made her uncomfortable, but she blamed it on nerves. She hoped the guy wasn't a cop.

As she picked up the menu, the perky waitress appeared at her table. "Can I start you off with coffee?"

"Sure...Dana." Willow read her name from the plastic tag on her breast. "That sounds perfect. Black." With another quick smile, Dana spun on her heel to fetch the coffee. Willow spied the bathrooms and slid out of the booth. She needed to check the mirror, something she should have done already. Next to the men's room, a payphone jutted from the wall. She considered it for a moment. The relic looked worn, but well maintained. When she was in on the streets in Philadelphia, she came across a few pay phones, even used a couple because she had no way of affording a cellphone right now.

Dipping into the women's restroom, she pulled her hood down to check her face. Tired, bruised eyes looked back at her. Hungry cheeks sank in more than usual. On one of them was a speck of red. In desperation, she washed it off with warm water. Then another on her forehead. She held her hands under the tap, scrubbing them and relishing the feel of the running water. Checking her hoodie, the black hid any spots.

She passed the payphone while exiting the restroom and pulled a couple quarters from her pocket. She needed to call someone. They needed to know it wasn't her fault.

As Willow pushed the coins into the slot, the metallic sound crashed in her ears. She checked to make sure no one was paying attention to her, but all the patrons were too busy with their own business to care.

She pressed each silver button, hoping she could remember the next digit of the phone number. There was a click and a buzz before someone picked up.

"Hello?"

"Cal, it's Willow."

"Wil! Where are you? I thought you were supposed to be-"

"I am," she interrupted him. "but I can't be for long. You were right, and I was wrong. Coming home was a bad idea. Nothing has changed." Her voice was low and even, though her hands shook as it held the receiver to her ear.

"I got a phone call from the cops. Did you go to Uncle Sean's house? Tell me you didn't because from what they told me..." he trailed off. She didn't blame him and wondered what the cops had told him. Regardless, she knew what she left behind when she ran from her uncle's home.

"He left me no choice." She whispered. "I didn't want to. I heard he stopped drinking and got help for his addictions."

"That's what *he* said, but no one believed him. He never was one for battling his demons. He'd rather take them out on everyone else," Cal said, the pain of his own memories in his voice. "Why did you even go there?"

"I had no other options. I'm on the street, Cal. You know that. You and Sean are all I have left of family. I figured if I could get a ride from Uncle Sean to get to you, I'd be okay."

"Wil, I'm sorry. You said you were heading out this way, but I didn't expect you to crash here. I mean, it's fine, but..." Cal's hesitation made her wonder if making this phone call was at all worth it. "The cops told me what happened. Did you do all of that to Sean and Barry?"

Willow was quiet. She didn't want to admit to anything over the phone, for one. Also, Cal's voice crackled and faded. Something was weird here and if it wasn't for the fact she was cold and hungry, she'd run out of this diner right now.

"Wil?"

"Yeah, sorry. I have to get out of here. I'll talk to you later." She pulled the handset away to hang it up, but Cal's voice brought it back to her ear.

"Wil. I have a buddy who still lives in the area. He can get you out of town. You can trust him. His name is Jason. He's a good guy. Where are you at?"

Willow said nothing at first. Street born paranoia served her well so far, but there were few options left. With only enough money for some food, any other transportation was out of the question.

"Queen City Diner. On Lehigh Street. It's funny that I found it. I haven't been here in years, and I feel like it called to me. Last time I was here, we were teenagers. Before you headed upstate."

"Wil. You're turned around. It can't be the Queen City." Cal said.

"The hell it ain't. I know where I'm at. I saw the sign outside. It's as I remembered it. I plan on drowning some waffles in syrup."

"Wil, you can't be at the Queen City Diner. They tore it down a couple years ago. I saw the empty lot myself when I was in town a month ago." Cal said. "You using again?"

"Fuck that." She said loud enough to elicit some stares from her fellow patrons.

The old man kept slurping his soup while the man at the counter continued eating his pie, though Willow had the distinct impression he heard every word of her conversation. Mother and toddler sat staring at each other. Willow turned away because it creeped her out too much.

"Fuck that," she repeated, whispering this time. "I've been clean since I broke up with Lynda. Maybe they rebuilt it. I don't know, but it is here. I'm standing in it."

"You need to get out of there." Cal said. The fear in his voice should have alerted Willow, but instead it agitated her. "Don't order a thing. Leave right now."

"Unless you told the cops where I am, I'm safe here. It's a good spot to lie low. Besides, I need to warm up." Willow's suspicion transformed into anger. "Don't mess with me. I'm out of options here. Please call your friend Jason. I need the ride out of here. If you don't want me at your house, I'll find someplace else to land."

The other side of the conversation was quiet for a moment. Finally, Cal said, choosing his words with deliberate care. "Okay. Fine, come here. I'll call him. But I can't tell him to pick you up at the diner. It's not there."

"I'm at the Queen City Diner. That's where he'll need to pick me up." Willow punctuated every word. "No cops Cal. I trust you. I want to warm up, eat, and get as far away as possible. Okay?"

Cal paused. "Okay. You can trust me. But seriously, Wil, get the hell out of there. I have a bad feeling."

There was a click, and the call cut off. Willow replaced the receiver, then hugged her hoodie tight against the chill crawling over her skin. As she passed the counter, she glanced at the man in the black coat. He kept his face turned away, suspiciously so. The older waitress gave a tired smile to Willow as they made eye contact. The smile was almost apologetic.

She returned to her booth, a steaming cup of coffee greeting her. She held it in both hands, soaking in its warmth. Before taking a sip, she sat it down and pressed the palm of her hands to her eyes. Exhaustion cascaded through her body, invading every pore. Behind her eyes, she saw blood. The back of Uncle Sean's head was deep red. The blood staining his thin blonde hair. Next to him lay Barry, Sean's friend. Barry's face was collapsed in an even pulpier mess than the back of her uncle's head.

With a shuddering sigh, she pulled her hands away from her face, blinking away the images until clarity returned. Out the window, she watched for prowling cop cars but saw only an empty street. The haze outside grew thicker.

Willow picked up the menu. She could afford a plate of waffles, and they sounded perfect right now.

With practiced timing, Dana appeared at her table and asked if she was ready to order.

"Waffles please." Willow handed her the menu.

"Is it just you tonight?"

"Yeah, I'm meeting someone, but they aren't staying. Catching a ride with a friend," Willow said, already regretting saying too much. She can't seem suspicious. *Cal's friend had better come through, and soon.*

"He meeting you here?" Dana asked, a look of mild disbelief on her face.

"Yes. Why not?" Willow's chest grew tight as she switched back into defensive mode. Remembering her conversation with Cal, she wondered why everyone was acting weird about this place. "Seems like a good spot as any."

In an abrupt chirp, the toddler erupted in a hysterical laugh. High pitched, it grated on her nerves. It grew manic and aggressive. The mother looked bemused, as if her child found a small wonder in the world and expressed newfound joy in it. Willow wanted to press her hands to her ears to drown it out. It traveled up her spine. The longer it continued, the more she wanted to scream.

Then, just as abrupt, the child stopped. Red faced and serious, he turned to her. Tear-wet eyes met hers. "It's for you," he said seconds before the pay phone's jarring ring filled the diner. Willow jumped, yelping in surprise at the sound. All the patrons faced to her. The old man even stopped slurping his soup to do so.

The phone continued ringing.

They continued to stare.

"I think it's for you," Dana whispered politely.

"Y-yeah. I guess I was the last one to use it." Willow slid out of the booth. The ringing wasn't as painful as the toddler's laugh, but still as disturbing. When she reached the phone, she carefully touched the receiver, almost as if it might bite her. She picked it up and looked back at the patrons before putting it to her ear. They continued to look at her. All but the man at the counter. He continued to eat his pie.

"Hello?" she whispered, her hand shaking.

"Wil? It's Cal. Where the hell are you?"

"Cal." Relief washed away some of the fear. He was the familiar voice she needed. "Is your friend on the way? Please tell me he is." She whispered. Somehow, she knew no matter how low she spoke, the entire diner heard every word of her conversation. "How much longer?"

"Jason drove to the diner, or where it used to be. Nothing is there, only a dirt lot. They never rebuilt the Queen City. Where are you?" Cal repeated.

"I literally just got off the phone with you a minute ago. How did he have time to come around so fast? I would have seen him." Willow turned around to peer out the window and took a step backwards. The dining area was empty. All the people were gone, even the man at the counter eating his pie.

"Oh shit! Cal, they're gone! They're all gone! I gotta go. Tell your friend I'll be on the street nearby."

"Wil, the cops know you were at Uncle Sean's house. Tell them it was self-defense. Sean has a history. They'll believe you," Cal pleaded as his voice faded.

"It *was* self-defense!" Willow screamed into the phone. "I have to get out of here. Something is wrong with this place." She slammed the handset back on the cradle and raced through the dining room to retrieve her backpack. As she reached her seat, something crashed in the kitchen. The lights dimmed, throwing everything into shades of gray and deep blue. Bag in hand, she spun around. From behind the serving window loomed a tall, monstrous figure with shining eyes. Its long misshapen face sprouted thin wiry hairs. It opened its mouth to reveal tombstone teeth. It growled at her.

Willow sprinted for the exit. "You haven't eaten your waffles yet." The man in the black coat reappeared at the counter. This time he faced her, but he didn't have a face, just a black starry void where it should have been. Willow spun and slammed into the front the door. It refused to budge. Dana stood behind it, the right side of her face caved in. Her bloody hands pressed against the glass, preventing it from opening.

"Sorry. Really, I am," the waitress apologized. Willow slammed into it again, this time putting her shoulder into it. The only thing she accomplished was creating a sharp pain down her arm. She heard something wet behind her. The old man was back, eating his soup. He watched her with silver eyes as he ate.

"I have to finish my soup. Can't leave until I finish my soup." He said in a phlegmy voice.

"Might as well get something to eat. You aren't going anywhere for a while." The man in the black coat said. At her booth sat a plate of waffles, rivulets of butter melting into the squares. A selection of syrups sat next to the plate.

The creature in the kitchen disappeared, but she could hear it lumbering around. Dana still stood at the door, looking sorry. Desperation clawed at Willow. Full panic threatened to consume her over-amped nervous system. Her night jumped from nightmare to nightmare. First her uncle and now this.

She eyed the restrooms, but that wasn't a way out. She needed an exit. In the back corner, on the other side of the kitchen, was a door. She prayed it led to an escape, and she bolted for it. No one stopped her as she slammed through it.

A bone chilling wind wrapped around her as everything went black. Her momentum carried her forward into the blackness until she stopped in a familiar living room.

"No," she whispered. "Not again."

"Wasn't expecting company," Uncle Sean said as Willow watched him open the front door of his house. She lived this scene before, only a short time ago. This time, she was an unseen observer.

"I know, I'm sorry, but I just got into town, and I don't have a phone to call ahead." Willow watched herself on Sean's step, apologizing for bothering him so late. From her angle, as she rewatched a scene she already lived through, she could see Sean's distrust with every word she said. He was aware she lived on the streets. He wasn't expecting her to show up on his doorstep.

Sean looked over his shoulder at the laptop sitting on the cluttered coffee table. "Come on in out of the cold." He opened the door and then went back to the laptop and folded the screen down. "Excuse the mess."

Willow could see what was on the laptop this time. It turned her stomach.

She saw her past-self walk in, nervous yet relieved to be indoors. "Leave. Get out of here!" She screamed at the doppelgänger. It went unacknowledged.

The living room was typical Sean, piles and stacks everywhere. Baseball memorabilia hung on the walls. It smelled of feet and citrus. Uncle Sean nervously explained his friend Barry was coming over. "You remember Barry, right?"

"Yeah, I remember him. Sorry, I need a place for the night, I swear, and I'll be out of your hair in the morning." The other Willow said, hoping not to get thrown out on the street. He looked her up and down. His breath was heavy with beer.

"Sure. I think we can arrange something. You hungry? Thirsty? You need anything else? Barry is bringing some 'party favors'," he said. The other Willow stepped back. Between his breath and his uncomfortable stares, she was already regretting this.

"No party favors for me. I've been clean for a while. Right now, I need to use your bathroom."

Willow followed a few steps behind herself to the bathroom. "We have to go. Maybe we can do it different this time. Please, go now." Willow pleaded with the memory, but to no avail. Her voice went unheard.

Someone knocked on the front door. Willow left Past-Willow to use the bathroom and returned to the living room. Sean opened the door to reveal Barry and a girl, who could have been either side of eighteen years old. She wore a swimmy look, and her steps were unsteady enough that Barry half-carried her inside.

"Told you I'd come through." Barry said with a smile. His youthful looks and athletic build were a contrast to his friend's. With a nudge, he pushed the girl through the doorway. In his hand was a fanny pack. He tossed it to Sean. "I brought 'snacks' for later. Turns out she likes pills." Willow stood helpless, unable to change anything.

Past-Willow came out of the bathroom.

"Hey, didn't realize you were bringing a playmate, too." Barry's smile made her skin crawl as he addressed her uncle.

"You remember my niece, Willow? She stopped by. Unexpectedly." Sean said, pointedly.

"You dirty bastard." Barry guffawed. Sean looked his niece up and down, then the other girl. He shrugged and reached for a bottle of beer on the coffee table and took a swig. "Maybe I am."

The girl looked at both men, and then at Willow. "Wait a minute. What's really going on?" She slurred. "You said this party was bumpin'."

"It is. Or at least it will be soon." Barry looked down at her as she took a step back.

"Take me back to the club. This ain't right." She slurred. The next set of actions were a blur. Willow didn't want to see it again, but she couldn't turn away either. The girl ran for the door, but Barry stopped her. Sean rounded on Past-Willow and threatened her to keep her mouth shut. "After all, you've probably done worse to survive on the streets. You can join in if you want." Her stomach turned at the words. "In fact, I really think you should."

Willow continued to watch the girl's limp attempts to claw and hit Barry, who only laughed and threw her to the floor. Sean forgot about his niece for the moment as he joined in his friend's laughter, his hand already on his zipper. The past-Willow looked around and saw a baseball bat hanging on the wall. At the sweet spot, some baseball player she didn't care about squiggled a signature on it. She pulled the bat off the wall.

The bat connected with her uncle's head. A sickening crack stopped all motion in the room. Barry roared at her and lunged. The reward for his action was the signature side of the bat to his face. He collapsed to the grimy carpet and Willow heaved the slugger over her head before bringing it down twice more with all her might. She spun around and did the same to the back of Sean's head before staggering back, panting.

The girl screamed and scrambled to her feet. She struggled with the doorknob before getting it open and stumbling into the night. The door slammed shut after her. Past-Willow watched her leave, then turned to her audience of one. Her eyes shone silver as she still gripped the wooden bat. "How else would one deal with this situation? Just run away into the night? You'd let a girl get raped by two pervy old men?"

"N-no. But it's murder." Willow said to her memory self. "I don't want to go to jail. There had to be another way."

The other Willow hefted the bat onto her shoulder, the silver eyes locking onto hers. "Murder is fun. Especially when it's horrible people." She snarled, showing tombstone teeth.

Willow backed away. On the floor, Sean's dead eyes stared at her. She yelped when he blinked. His eyes also showed silver.

"She's safe now, right? That's what counts." Willow hoped it was the case.

"Are you safe now? She's alone in the night. Just like you." The memory-Willow stretched and grew, her legs cracking backwards at the knees and face stretching down to a pointed chin. "C'mere."

Somewhere, Willow heard slurping sounds. She spun around and grabbed the doorknob. Behind her, the creature snarled. Willow ducked in time, the bat catching the door and wrenching it from her hands. Splinters from the door rained down on her before it slammed shut. Willow ducked again, rushing past this thing masquerading as her. She bolted down the hallway and into the bathroom...

...and ran right back into the empty diner.

Nothing followed her. The creature was gone.

She fought disorientation both from the sudden shift in realities, but also because the colors of the diner had been reversed. Before, what was bathed in gray light was blue shadow and vice versa. All the seats were empty. Or so it seemed. She ran for the exit.

Standing at the cash register was the older waitress, smoking a cigarette. "Might as well eat your waffles, hon. No sense going hungry." As she smoked, blood dripped from her nose and left ear. Her eyes were silver.

"You're all dead, aren't you?" Willow whimpered.

"Leroy, the cook, said you weren't bright, but I argued otherwise. I could tell you were sharp, just tired." The waitress said, stepping away. "Leroy is an ass, anyway. Ask Dana. She can tell you all about it." She pointed to her head, in the same place Dana's was caved in. The thing in the kitchen grunted.

"What do you want? Please, let me go!" Willow backed up.

"Have something to eat and take a load off." The man in the black coat said, resuming his assault on his pie. The room swam in front of Willow. She would have fallen if the older waitress hadn't taken her arm to balance her. Willow took her arm away and leaned against the back of the nearest booth.

"Just sit, dear. You're in no condition." The mother tutted as she wiped sticky pancake from her toddler's mouth.

"Once I finish my soup, I can leave." The old man said between spoonfuls.

"Leroy! Order up." The waitress walked towards the kitchen as the monstrous cook plated food.

"Sit. You're in no shape to travel." The man in the black coat said, his void-face turned towards. Willow did as she was told. Tired, scared, confused, and disoriented; she had few other options. The couple was sitting across from her again. Both men looking at each other with longing, gripping each other tight. So tight they became one. Their arms melded into each other like warm putty.

The old woman also returned, her scowl deepening to an almost comical degree. Hate and disgust radiated out like a physical force. Air shimmered and warped between the two booths. Invisible heat rushed towards them, and the boys smoldered and caught fire. Still lost in each other's eyes, they smiled, oblivious to the immolation. They burned unharmed. The old woman, her eyes shining silver, admired the fire and waited for destruction.

"Here, hon." Dana approached with a fresh plate in one hand and a full carafe of coffee in the other. The wound at her temple wept blood onto her shoulder. She filled Willow's cup and set the plate of waffles down. "Eat up." Her voice said cheerily, but her eyes filled with regret.

Willow did nothing at first. She merely observed. The man at the counter ate his pie, the old man ate his soup. The toddler's face was still sticky with syrup. The monster in the kitchen worked. The two waitresses stood at the counter, wiping glasses and filling napkin holders.

The teens burned.

The old woman scowled.

The mother doted on her child.

Willow watched.

The woman scowled.

The teens burned.

The child ate.

The waitresses bled.

The men ate.

The cook prepped.

Willow watched.

The boys didn't die as they burned.

The waitresses didn't die as they bled.

The child continued to eat.

The mother continued to coddle.

The void-faced man always had pie.

The old man never stopped his incessant slurping.

Willow understood.

She stood up, leaving her coffee and waffles untouched. She walked up to the old man. He looked up at her, spoon of watery soup at his lips. Taking his bowl in her hands, she slid it from under him and chucked it across the room. It splashed on the nearby tables before the bowl shattered against the counter next to the man and his pie. He didn't even flinch.

"I guess I'm done with my soup." The old man said. He pulled a crumpled five-dollar bill from his sweater and laid it on the table, careful to set his sweating water glass on the corner of it. He slid out arthritically from his booth and walked out the door.

Willow approached the toddler. She put her hand on his plate, but the mother put her hand on Willow's, stopping her.

"It's a little late for pancakes, don't you think?" Willow asked her.

"You don't understand. He's a growing boy. And he can't leave now. Not without finishing his pancakes. And I can't leave him." The mother pleaded. "You understand, don't you?"

"I think I do." Willow said, stepping away. The couple still melted together, still burned, but the fire wasn't the same. It wasn't from the hateful old woman; it was a fire of their own making now.

"I'm sorry, but I don't want to be stuck here like you people. I need to go," Willow said, walked towards the door again.

"What do you have to go out there for? It's cold and you have nowhere to go. Even your cousin isn't sure if he wants you around. You're home-less, broke, and on the run." The void-faced man said, turning towards her. She looked away, unable to handle his endlessness. "Besides, you're a murderer now. Might as well stay here with the rest of us. All these people have chosen to stay. We aren't alone here. That's why I invited them all. Same as I invite you."

"This is a horror show. You're not inviting me. You're using my trauma against me, tricking me to stay."

"Where will you go?" the toddler asked, his small voice earnest.

"You're all dead." Willow stepped back. "I'll take my chances out there." She turned and lunged for the door. With all her might, she slammed into it. The door chimed as she fell into a blinding light and the sound of screeching brakes.

She blinked and jumped back. A car bumper and the rumble of an engine were inches from her knees. She held up her hand to block out the light.

"Hey! Are you Willow?" A bearded man in glasses poked his head out of the driver's side window. "I've been looking all over for you. Cal sent me."

"You're Jason?" Willow backed away from the car. "Take off your glasses. Let me see your eyes." She insisted and kept insisting until he complied. Satisfied his eyes weren't shining silver, she slid into the passenger's seat. The warmth of the heater caused her skin to prickle.

"Cal told me you were at the Queen City and I told him he was nuts. The place hasn't been around for years. He said you needed a lift pretty bad, so I've been driving up and down the street. Figured I'd park here for a minute since he said you were pretty insistent about being at the diner. Didn't expect you to hop out of nowhere like that. Kinda creepy, honestly." He said.

Willow looked out the windshield. The lot in front of them was empty of everything but some dancing plastic bags and a rolling A-Treat bottle. She didn't bother asking where the diner had gone. She already knew.

He put the car in reverse and backed out. "Am I taking you to Cal's?"

"I don't care where you take me. I just want to get as far away from this fucking place as I possibly can." Willow said. As they drove off, she watched haze cling to the side of a building that was no longer there.

9

TELL ME HOW YOU DIED

BY D. A. LATHAM

"Tell me how you died."

She waited for the woman to answer. They always took so long to answer. Maybe they didn't want to relive the last moments of their lives. Maybe they couldn't remember right away. She was patient, though. The moon was high and the air cool. She would wait as long as she needed to get the answers.

Bella loved Queen Street Cemetery. It had been around long before the city became a city. Over the years, it grew acre by acre until progress halted its growth with asphalt and multi-level houses. The newest graves were closer to the street, while the older graves, the ones that Bella often visited, were in the back, near the woods.

When her family moved to their house on Queen Street, Bella was instantly fascinated with the cemetery at the end of the street. Her mother wasn't too thrilled to be living close to a cemetery, but Bella's parents couldn't beat the price of the home they purchased.

The first Saturday after they had moved in, Bella went for a walk and ended up opening the rusted gate and walking slowly through the rows of gravestones. She read as many as she could, noting names and dates. She found those who died in their old age, those who died in childhood and those who died in the prime of their lives. She became curious about how these people died.

Did they die in their sleep from a heart attack? An unfortunate accident? Murder? Bella became captivated by the possibilities. She became obsessed with finding out the answers.

Hours were spent at the library poring over old records and newspaper articles. The results were unsatisfying. She wanted to gritty details, not the glossed over reports she found. She wanted to know how the deceased felt when they realized they were dying. What the pain felt like. Did they see the famous "light" as their heart stopped beating?

Bella changed her research tactic, instead of reading police and autopsy reports, she started reading books on witchcraft and the occult. It was amazing the information you could find in old dusty books stored away in the back rooms of libraries. She found a ritual that would allow her to communicate with the dead. It would bring them back long enough for her to get the information she so desperately wanted.

After obtaining the items outlined in the ritual she had found, Bella left her house and walked to the end of the street. She opened the rusted gate of Queen Street Cemetery and walked through the quiet graveyard, searching for a grave to visit. After wandering the rows of stones, she found a grave with the name Johnathan Harlin, born 1885, died 1905. Perfect for a first try.

Bella placed the black rose on top of the grave. Sitting down, she pulled out the small pocketknife and sliced her thumb. A trickle of warm blood dripped onto the rose as she recited the words from the book. She sat back and waited for the magic to work.

Minutes passed, and she began to think that it was a crock of shit.

"Ugh. I knew magic wasn't real." She huffed.

But then she heard a soft humming sound. Bella looked around to see if there was someone nearby. She couldn't see much in the darkness.

The air over Jonathan Harlin's grave started to shimmer. Eyes widening, Bella scrambled back from the grave. A tiny rumble of the ground and the earth split a little. A puff of smoke rose from the opening in the grave. It swirled in a small vortex above Jonathan's grave and slowly took the shape of a young man.

Jonathan Harlin raised his transparent arms and brought them to his face. It was his face that gave a clue to how he died. The left side of this face was perfect. Unblemished skin, dark arched eyebrow over a sky blue eye. The right side, the right side of his face, was crushed in. Blood and brain matter squeezed out of his ear and was matted in his beard and hair. The eye on that side hung from the optical nerve and was shriveled up like a raisin and resting on his ruined cheek.

"Tell me how you died, Jonathan." Bella whispered.

Jonathan touched the right side of his head gingerly and pulled away his ghostly fingers, looking at the blood that shimmered in the moonlight with his one good eye.

He spent a long time feeling around his face. The good side and the pulverized right side almost as if he were comparing them to each other and trying to figure out what was happening. Time passed and Bella thought for sure he wasn't going to answer. She was frustrated that there was nothing she could do but wait.

He looked at Bella and began to tell his story. Because half his mouth was destroyed, his words were a little slurred.

"My father had bought a new horse for our farm. A beautiful sorrel stallion 15 hands high named Oscar. It was wild. The family Father bought it from did not train it. He thought it would be a good idea for me to break the beast. If I was ale to, he said the horse could be mine. I spent weeks grooming it so it would get used to me. I would feed it apples as a treat after. I thought for sure I was getting through to it." He shook his head.

"After a month, I decided it was time to try to ride him. I laid a blanket over his back and placed the saddle and bridle on him. I spoke soothing words to him as I got into the saddle. I rubbed his neck when I was finally seated with my feet in the stirrups. I started him off at a slow trot, but when I dug my heels into his sides to get him to move faster, he reared up and I fell off, landing in the dirt on my arm. A loud *crack as* my arm shattered made me scream, which frightened the horse. Holding my injured arm, I looked up and all I could see were hooves above my head. The horse was snorting, and it's eyes were rolling back in its head. "

"I tried to protect myself, tried to roll out of the way shouting for help. Oscar stomped on my side. I heard my ribs crack. It felt like knives piercing my chest as the bones poked through my skin, ripping my shirt open. Its hooves crushed my knees, bending them backwards. The pain flowed through my body like lightning. I couldn't move. All I could do is scream."

"The last thing I remember is watching Oscar's hooves coming toward my face. I heard a loud wet crunch and everything went black.

Bella smiled when Jonathan finished his story.

"Thank you, Jonathan. You can go now." She said. As soon as the words left her mouth, Jonathan's form disappeared back into his grave.

The first taste of the truth of death made Bella hungry. Hungry to devour more death stories. She returned home and sat at the desk in her bedroom. The light from her laptop illuminating her face as she typed out the details of Jonathan Harlin's death. This would be the most gruesome journal. And now she had to plan on who was going to go next. At the library, she had written down some names of those buried in Queen Street Cemetery. Looking through that list, she decided her next interview would be Cady Bowles. Born 1975, died 2001.

The black rose shriveled, the smoke rose from the damp ground and Cady Bowles appeared above her grave. Her long brown hair floated around her head as if she was underwater. Her jeans and t-shirt were stained scarlet. The color radiating out from a large wound in her abdomen.

"Tell me how you died Cady."

Cady cocked her head to the side as she looked at Bella. Hands clutching her stomach. Her ethereal body twitched and jerked. Bella knew that it would take a bit for the ghost to answer her. She sat cross-legged on the cool grass with her hands resting on her knees and watched Cady float next to her gravestone.

Ten minutes became twenty. Twenty minutes became thirty. Finally, Cady launched into her story.

"I drove too fast." She answered in a high, childlike voice. "Went out to celebrate getting a new job. Met a group of friends at The Walnut down on Main St. We played darts, drank a lot of shots. My bestie Lisa asked me not to drive home, but I promised her I was just fine to drive."

"Old Hollow Rd has a lot of twists and turns, you know. My foot was heavy on the gas pedal. I remember signing along to Lady Marmalade by Christina Aguilera at the top of my lungs and laughing. With this new job, nothing was going to stop me! But, then a deer ran out in front of my car. I swerved to get around it, but it got spooked and jumped right into my car. I slammed on the brakes, but not soon enough. The front end of my car slammed into a tree, the deer's head shattered the windshield and I blacked out."

"When I came to, all I could see was brown fur and antlers. I could hear huffing breaths from the deer. It took me a while to figure out why I couldn't move. Its antlers had driven through my stomach and pinned me to the seat of my car. I tried so hard to push it off the hood, but it was too heavy. It thrashed its head, trying to free itself, and I could feel the sharp points of its antlers scrambling my insides. I screamed as my blood soaked into my clothes."

"The deer and I died together slowly. It took hours. Every once in a while, it would struggle. I could hear its hooves clattering against the hood. Like death bells announcing the end. It's not like the movies or in books where they say you see your life flash before your eyes. Pain, that's what the end was like. Pain that lit up every single nerve in my body. I pissed myself, and I felt my bowels let go."

"Dying was kind of easy, I guess. I just closed my eyes and felt the world slip away." Cady probed the wound in her stomach, pushing her fingers inside the moist, gory hole. "Huh, I guess that sucker got me good. I can almost get my whole hand inside!"

Bella gagged a little, watching Cady explore her abdomen from the inside. "Thank you, Cady. You can go now."

Cady smiled and gave a little wave as she disintegrated back to the other side.

Bella didn't know quite what to make of Cady's story. She didn't realize the dead could have such a positive look at how they died. She guessed that maybe it was the fact that even though Cady died in a horrific accident, she had been happy and carefree right before it happened.

After talking with Cady, Bella walked home and tried to avoid her mother when she went inside. Her mom didn't like the fact that Bella spent so much time in the cemetery. Her mother and father wanted her to start therapy, but she told them that spending time in the cemetery was all the therapy she needed. Of course, she didn't tell them exactly what she was doing there[CN1] [DL2] . It was best if they believed she just liked to walk around in there and look at the gravestones. They knew that Queen Street Cemetery had been around for a long time, so some of the graves were from the 1800s.

The next person on the list that Bella wanted to speak to was Olsen Martins. Born 1965. Died 1998. She was especially excited to talk with Olsen. He had been the victim of a serial killer. The police report she had read on the murder gave a few details of the way in which he was killed. Bella knew there was way more to it than what was documented. There had to be.

She placed the black rose on his grave.

She cut her thumb with the pocketknife and let her blood drip onto the rose.

She recited the words she now had memorized.

Olsen's grave shimmered and the ground split. Smoke rose and formed into Olsen Martins.

"Tell me how you died Olsen." Bella asked breathlessly. She knew this was going to be the best account of death yet.

Like the others, Olsen took his time to answer. His mouth opened a closed several times. His eyes darted left and right as if he was looking for someone or something, like he was nervous. Tears started to flow from his eyes.

"I was walking home from work. I liked to walk, and it wasn't far from my job. The exercise was good for me. One night, though, I didn't make it back home. A guy was following me. I tried to ignore him. Thought maybe it was my imagination that I was being followed. Or maybe I was just being paranoid. I decided to cut down an alley to get home faster, and that's when he ran up behind me. He wrapped one arm around my neck and the other held a cloth to my face. There was a weird smell on the rag and next thing I knew, I was waking up in a dark room that smelled like mold and copper."

"My head hurt when I woke up. It was cold and damp and I couldn't stop shivering. I yelled out, asking if anyone was there to help me. Suddenly, a light turned on, blinding me. I heard a door slam open and footsteps coming downstairs. The man that came into my view was wearing a mask. 'Oh, you're awake now,' he said to me. I begged him to let me go. But he told me that wasn't an option."

"I pissed myself. I was so scared when I saw him pull out a hunting knife. He started cutting my shirt off and made fun of me because I was crying and begging. He told me to 'man up and stop whining' and that it would only hurt for a few hours. After he got my shirt off, he stabbed me right beneath my Adam's apple. The man gripped the knife handle with both hands and tugged it down. I could hear my skin ripping. It sounded like fabric being torn. He dragged the knife down my torso, stopping at my waist. He dropped the knife and reached into my body. His fingers dug into the wound and gripped the first organ he could. With several yanks, I looked down and saw my intestines lying on my lap. I remember he laughed then. Laughed like a lunatic as he reached back inside. Organ by organ, he emptied my abdomen. Stomach, spleen, kidneys. All pulled out. No one should have to look at their own viscera. I wanted to look away, but I couldn't."

"I guess I was in shock. After a while, I couldn't feel anything. I just watched as my life flowed out of me in crimson torrents, splattering the man's shirt. His arms and hands were stained with my blood. I felt my heartbeat getting slower and slower as I watched the man reach inside one more time. He clutched my heart in his fist and yanked."

"That's the last thing I remember."

Bella smiled. "Thank you, Olsen. You can go now."

For years, Queen Street Cemetery kept Bella company with the ghosts she forced back to the land of the living to get the most intimate details of their deaths. She kept going until it came time for her to go to college. Luckily, there was a cemetery near her school, so she was still able to indulge in her morbid hobby.

. Her mother had died two years ago and each year on the anniversary he throws a celebration of life party to remember his late wife. Bella didn't like coming home for these celebrations, but she did to keep up appearances. She was only home for a few days, so she had to make sure she visited her favorite place at least one time before going back to college. The celebration had ended a few hours ago and she was finally able to go to Queen Street cemetery.

The woman stared at her before her story started to flow from lips that were bloated and blue. The woman's skin was a sickly green color and looked like it would rupture at any time.

"I drowned," the woman said. "My family and I were out on a boat that we rented from the campground we were staying at. We went there every summer. Every summer, we rented the same boat that we would take out on the lake and spend the day. The sun was shining, we had the music playing loud and were just enjoying being together. My oldest daughter made lunch for everyone before we had left that morning, so she was in charge of passing out the sandwiches and drinks. It made me so happy to see her participating. Usually, she is grumpy and withdrawn during our family trips. After we ate lunch, we all became sleepy. It wasn't long before we were all asleep."

"All of us except my oldest daughter. She pushed me out of the boat into the water. I didn't wake up fully, but I was aware enough to feel each breath I took pull water into my lungs. I couldn't help but scream and draw more water into my lungs, even though I knew it was going to kill me. Everything was silent as all the air in my lungs was finally replaced by water."

Bella clapped her hands in delight. Hearing this story was the best ever. She wondered what she would have to do to get a better story.

"Thank you, Mom. You can go now."

10

— · —

QUEENIE

BY ASHLEY LISTER

"BECAUSE OF QUEENIE."

Mike frowned at the response, wondering if he'd heard correctly. The reception area of the Golden Years Care Home was surprisingly noisy this lunchtime, making it difficult for him to hear the softly spoken man in the wheelchair. It was the weekend before Christmas and a handful of families had come to visit some of the elderly residents. Mike cautioned himself to use the word 'residents' in his thoughts, rather than 'inmates' as he knew it would only take one slip of the tongue like that in front of the care home's ball-busting manager and he'd find himself unemployed again.

"Say that again, Mr Winters," he insisted. He raised his voice so there was less chance of the elderly man mishearing because of the potentially confusing sounds around them. "I was asking: how come you were moving into your fifth care home this year? You're not a trouble-causer, are you?" He asked this last question with a laugh, to show that it was meant in a spirit of fun.

"It's because of Queenie," Mr Winters repeated. "She shows up, and it means I have to leave." Lowering his voice to a conspiratorial whisper, he added, "She follows me."

"Queenie," Mike repeated. "Is she a friend? A member of your family? Someone dangerous?" He left the three suggestions hanging there, knowing that Mr Winters would fill the silence.

"Queenie's a ghost," Mr Winters said.

Mike nodded sympathetically and kept his features poker-player fixed. "A ghost," he agreed. At the back of his mind, he was thinking he needed to inform the manager of Golden Years Care Home that their latest resident might be showing signs of mental decline. It wasn't that he disbelieved in ghosts, but, if he was taking a bet on the probability of this case, it was more likely that he was talking to a deluded old man rather than someone with a genuine connection to the spirit world.

He got Mr Winters settled into his room, a second floor single near the fire escape, and went to talk with Tanya Hide, the manager. The woman wasn't really called Tanya Hide, which Mike thought was a name he'd heard on an episode of *Drag Race*. Her real name was Tonya Heidelberg, but Mike thought it amusing to think of her as someone with the identity of a cartoonish S&M disciplinarian. Again, he inwardly cautioned himself against the flippant use of a wrong word because, he knew, if he made a mistake with her name, especially in front of the woman, she'd see he no longer had a job.

"Tanya," he began, after knocking on her open door and stepping inside.

"Tonya," she corrected.

He winced at his own stupidity and apologised. Tonya Heidelberg wore a suit, a professional smile and a corporate lanyard. She had dark hair, dark eyes, skin the colour of an autopsy, and a thinly disguised hatred for Mike. Her office was neat to the point of a pathological condition, which always made Mike feel as though he was a piece of unwanted rubbish that needed to be removed from her presence.

"I've just settled a new resident into his room," Mike began, "and I was worried that he might be displaying signs of confusion."

"Signs of confusion?" Tonya smiled. "Did he, perhaps, get your name wrong?"

Mike kept his smile fixed, figuring he deserved that jibe, and said stiffly, "He said he's being followed by a ghost."

Tonya raised an eyebrow and Mike recounted the exchange he'd had with Mr Winters. She nodded solemnly and said, "Thank you for bringing this to my attention, Michael. I shall make a note of it now."

She picked up a pen from her desk and began to write on a pus-yellow Post-It note. She said the words aloud as she wrote them and, at first, Mike assumed this was so he could see she was taking his observation seriously.

"New resident is displaying signs of delusion and confusion, *according to our resident expert on mental health in the elderly*." She paused theatrically and said, "No. I need to correct that last part. You're not our resident expert on mental health in the elderly, are you? *According to our minimum wage probationary porter*." Her smile was gone as she glared at Mike and said, "Is there anything else, Michael?"

He shook his head and left the office, inwardly telling himself that Tanya Hide was a fucking bitch. It wasn't the first time he'd come away with such an opinion of the woman and he suspected, one day, he was going to tell her as much. However, he figured such an exchange was likely to occur on his last day working at the Golden Years Care Home and, if he wanted to continue paying his rent and chipping away at the debt on his credit cards, he needed to keep hold of this job until something better came along. All of which meant putting up with Tanya's rudeness, enduring her hostility, and not complaining later that day when she sent word that he would be covering the nightshift for the foreseeable future.

Mike didn't mind the change from working days to working nights. The Golden Years Care Home was quieter on an evening. There were less chores to be done, and Tanya Hide was usually headed for home, an hour after his shift had started, so that meant Mike had less time to endure her toxicity. It also meant that he had more time to chat with patients and other staff members and, as a self-confessed people person, that was almost as good as receiving a cash bonus.

Almost.

Because Tonya had made sure he was working through most of the Christmas holidays and covering for any unexpected staff absences, the change in his routine gave Mike a chance to quickly become a recognised and trusted face amongst the other nightshift workers. This was how he ended up having a midnight coffee and a smoke with Connie from the second floor on one of the first nights of the new year.

They were standing outside the kitchen door, an unofficial designated smoking area for staff members at the Golden Years Care Home. The chill night air was lit by a monstrously bright motion detector light that exterminated the night's darkness. It was bright enough for Mike to see the ghosts of his words take shape with every exhalation.

"How's Mr Winters settling in?" he asked.

"The second floor single near the fire escape?" Connie asked guardedly. "He seems OK."

There was something in the way that she said the words that made Mike believe everything was not OK. Usually, residents were discussed in terms of hyperbolic praise and superlatives. Old Mrs Shelby was described as 'the sweetest', even though they all knew she regularly referred to her granddaughter as 'a poisonous little cunt'. Dr Patterson was described as 'the most charming and polite', even though it was common knowledge that he kept asking the young female volunteers for hand-jobs or a titty-wank. From Mike's limited experience in dealing with residents at the Golden Years Care Home, OK was seldom OK.

"Is he presenting problems?" he asked.

"What's your interest?"

"I met him on his first day," Mike explained. "He seemed pleasant enough, but he's got a history of being passed from one care home to another. I just wondered if he was settled now, or if he was likely to move on." He thought of mentioning the comment about Queenie, the ghost that Mr Winters believed was following him, but Tonya Heidelberg's scathing response to this observation made Mike hold his tongue.

"I don't think he's going to stay," Connie said eventually. "He's not playing well with the other puppies, and he's acting a little odd."

"Odd how?" Mike asked.

Connie considered this for a long moment as she drew on her smoke. "He closes his bedroom door by eight o'clock on an evening. Every evening. But he doesn't go to bed."

"What does he do?"

"He just sits in his armchair and stares at the door to the en-suite." She shook her head as though disagreeing with something Mike hadn't said and added, "I've stepped in a couple of times. My intention was just to make sure he was settled for the night but, instead of finding that he'd gone to bed, each time I've found him bolt upright, sitting in his chair." Lowering her voice, she added, "And it always looks like he's been glaring at the bathroom door."

Mike thought about this and agreed it was odd behaviour, but he wasn't sure that was enough to move Mr Winters into the realms of simply being 'OK'. "What else is it that's making you uneasy about him?"

"His room is always fricking cold," Connie admitted. "And I think that's a coldness he's brought with him."

Mike was thinking of those words an hour later when he was walking along the second-floor corridor and passing the door to Mr Winters' room. A prickle of goosebumps had crept up his forearm. He supposed it was one of the drawbacks to working the nightshift in a care home: the ghost stories eventually started getting to you.

He'd heard about an elderly woman nearing the end of her life at the Golden Years Care Home who had bitterly complained about the people in her bedroom. She said they surrounded her bed and glared at her and whispered that she should hurry up. The nurse who told him that story had said there was no one else in the room and Mike had been left with an image of ghostly psychopomps, figures from beyond the grave, waiting to escort the old woman to the halls of whichever geriatric Valhalla she was destined to visit. Even this evening, the idea of ghosts waiting around a deathbed was enough to make him shiver in a sweat of cold dread.

He'd heard about the war veteran, having a seizure in the same room where Mr Winters now resided, clutching at the attendant paramedic and saying, "You're next." The veteran had been twisted by repeated spasms, each one apparently more painful than the last. But, when he grabbed the arm of the paramedic and spoke, his voice had been calm and there had been no slurring of his speech as he said the words. "You're n ext."

From what Mike had been told, the paramedic quit his job the next day, and no one had heard from him since. But that left Mike wondering if the story was just a fiction with an inconclusive end, meant to scare newbies on the nightshift, or if, for some supernatural reason, the paramedic had really been the next to die and no one had been able to share that conclusion with the original narrator.

And now he was remembering his conversation with Connie, who had told him that Mr Winters sat up all night watching the door to his bathroom. She said he'd brought an inexplicable coldness with him, and Mike thought the image of the old man, sitting up all night and glaring at a bathroom door, was probably more haunting than any of the other stories he'd heard about the Golden Years Care Home.

He paused outside the door and wondered if he should do the responsible thing and check on Mr Winters. It wasn't technically one of the roles he was supposed to undertake during his nightshift hours, and he suspected that Tanya Hide would tear him a new arsehole if she found he had been using his initiative to do something for the benefit of a resident. But the idea of the elderly gentleman sitting awake and glaring at his bathroom door was too unsettling for Mike to let it slip from his thoughts without being addressed.

He knocked gently on the door: loud enough to be heard but quiet enough to not disturb the man's sleep if he had retired for the evening.

"Go away," Mr Winters said evenly. "It's one o'clock in the morning. Can't you leave an old man alone at this hour?"

Mike pushed the door open and grinned into the room.

As Connie had said he would be, Mr Winters was sitting in a chair facing the bathroom door. He was dressed in the typical geriatric fashions of sliders, sweatpants, and a shapeless hoodie. These were clothes that didn't demand dextrous fingers to fasten clasps, operate zips, or tie laces. This beige ensemble was made up of clothes that were elasticated and easy to slide on and off. The outfit carried all the dignity and sophistication of the wardrobe used by toddlers. And all of these weary, shapeless garments were hidden beneath a tartan blanket that Mr Winters had draped over his shoulders to ward off the room's pressing cold.

"You're awake," Mike observed.

"What do you want, Mark?"

Mike didn't bother correcting the wrong name. "Connie said you'd been having difficulty sleeping. I just came in to see if there was anything I could help with."

Mr Winters raised a sceptical eyebrow. "Connie said, I'd 'been having difficulty sleeping,'" he repeated.

Mike shrugged. "I'm paraphrasing," he admitted. "But it looks like she was right, doesn't it? You're not in bed. You're sitting up in your chair, and you look like you're wide awake to me. Is there anything I can help with? Or is there anything you want to talk about?"

Mr winters shook his head. "Talking won't do any good."

"Perhaps," Mike agreed. "But it's not likely to do any harm either, is it?"

Mr Winters released a heavy sigh. "Come in and take a seat, Mark," he grumbled. "But I'll warn you now, I've got little to say, and it's bloody cold in here."

Mike stepped into the room and settled himself on the unused bed. The old man was correct about the room's temperature. It was like stepping into one of the walk-in freezers they had in an industrial food-processing plant. He could see his breath each time he exhaled and, after only a moment inside the room, Mike felt his bones begin to tremble with the chill.

"How come you're staring at the bathroom doorway?" he asked.

"That's where she'll come from," Mr. Winters explained. His gaze had returned to the bathroom door. He didn't glance at Mike as he spoke. "That's where she always comes from."

Mike was going to ask who the old man was talking about when he remembered the first exchange he'd had with the old man. "Is it Queenie?"

"That's her," Mr Winters agreed. "She's been coming for me for a while now, and she always comes from the bathroom."

"Who is she?" There was a long silence. For an instant, Mike started to wonder if Mr Winters hadn't heard the question or had possibly dropped into a sleep where his eyes remained open and fixed on the unmoving handle of the bathroom door. Raising his voice slightly, he asked again, "Who is she?"

"Do you believe in ghosts?" Mr Winters asked.

Mike thought about this before answering. "I don't believe in ghosts during the day," he admitted. "But at this time of night, during the long hours of winter, my scepticism isn't quite so self-assured."

Mr Winters grunted dry amusement. "I don't believe in ghosts," he said calmly. He continued to glare at the door as he added, "But I do believe in vengeful spirits."

"Is Queenie a vengeful spirit?"

"She has every reason to be."

"What happened?"

Again, the old man fell silent, and Mike was left with the certainty that the man wasn't going to answer his question. He had a moment to reflect on the cold in the room, which was more intense than could have been expected. Admittedly, the night outside was cold. He had seen a sprinkling of snow on the ground whilst he'd been having a smoke with Connie, but this room was colder.

"Queenie and I had lived together for forty years," Mr Winters began. His voice was the measured drawl of a man who had been holding onto a secret for too long. "We were young and stupid and had our whole lives ahead of us and we vowed that we weren't going to end up as old farts in one of God's waiting rooms, like this one."

Mike nodded. He considered himself young enough to understand the mindset of fearing old age. If it was a choice between a short life filled with pleasure and hedonistic experience, and a long life made miserable by the trappings of age and infirmity, it seemed like a no-brainer as to which would be more desirable.

"So, we made a bargain," Mr Winters explained. "We came to an agreement that, if either one of us started showing signs of becoming an old fart, the other one would do the decent thing."

Mike held up a hand. He had several questions. The first was wondering how Mr Winters and Queenie had defined 'becoming an old fart'. Was that just down to a subjective judgement? Had someone become an old fart if they started to enjoy nine o'clock bedtimes, reruns of *Murder She Wrote*, or wearing a pair of comfy slippers? Or was the condition based on something more substantial, like a loss of mobility or a decline in mental faculties?

He also wanted to know what Mr Winters meant by 'the decent thing'. Did 'the decent thing' involve providing adequate medical care and appropriate material, as well as psychological and spiritual support? Or was it a poorly veiled euphemism for committing a mercy killing?

Mr Winters shook his head. "Ask your questions later, Mark," he insisted. "This is the first time I've ever spoken about this, so let me say what I've got to say first." He didn't shift his gaze from the door to the bathroom. He stared at it as though his life depended on holding the door shut with his merciless glare.

Mike nodded and settled back in his seat on the bed.

"It happened a couple of years ago," he explained. "There were a series of small things, forgetting names, losing keys and not remembering appointments and birthdays. She'd have been in her early sixties then. At the same time, she took a couple of falls, and that slowed her considerably. She was limping because of a replacement hip. She was slow, even with a cane. She had difficulty with stairs. And I realised she was showing all the signs of becoming an old fart. That meant I had to do the decent thing."

Mike leant closer.

Mr Winters kept his gaze fixed on the bathroom door as he spoke, spitting the words as though they were bullets that had needed firing for a long time. "Of course, I asked her if she was turning into an old fart. But she just laughed off the question. She'd say she wasn't a spring chicken any longer. She'd say she was just having a little bit of bad luck. She'd say she was having an off day. She'd say she was just feeling a little tired, and it was probably a passing thing. But, in her eyes, I could see the truth. In her eyes, I could see that she knew what she was becoming. And, in her eyes, I could see that she needed me to keep my promise and do the decent thing."

He fell silent for a moment.

It was long enough for Mike to hear the man's dentures chattering together through the cold. "What did you do?" Mike asked.

"She was relaxing in the bath one night," Mr Winters told him. "She was doing the thing with candles, bubbles, essential oils, and whale music. I crept in behind her and held her under the surface of the water." He paused and thought about this and then said, "She struggled a little. But it was only the struggling of an old fart."

The words hung heavily between them.

Mike wondered what he was supposed to do with a confession of murder. He couldn't imagine Tanya Hide being impressed with this development. She'd find some way of downgrading his duties to being the resident nightsoil man.

"The coroner concluded that it was an accidental death," Mr Winter continued. "But that wasn't the verdict that Queenie had reached. She came to me one night a month after she died. She was coming out of the bathroom, and she looked just the same as she had on the night when I killed her: wet, wrinkled and bedraggled." After a moment's reflection, he said, "Maybe not quite the same. Now she looked mightily pissed."

Mike shivered but said nothing.

"She opened the bathroom door and started toward me. She said, 'If it was my time, it's your time too.' Then she reached for me with both of her hands."

"What did you do?" asked Mike.

Mr Winters snatched his gaze away from the door and studied Mike quietly. "I did the only thing I could do," he admitted. "I ran. I ran out of that house and spent the night asleep in my car. The next day, I made arrangements to sell the house and tried to move into a different one. It took a week for that to happen. That was a week where I slept in my car every night. But once I'd moved into a new home, I discovered that Queenie wasn't confined to that one bathroom."

Mike said nothing.

"She came out of the bathroom at the new place, and I almost died from terror. I took the precaution of boarding up the bathroom door, but she wasn't going to let things like wood and nails stop her from bursting out and telling me it was my time. It was around then that I was committed to a psychiatric unit, where they thought I was carrying unresolved guilt for Queenie's untimely death." He laughed bitterly and said, "Since they made that genius observation, gave me a load of tablets and released me from their care, I've been shunting myself from one care home to another as I try to recuperate. But the sad thing is, Queenie can come out of any bathroom she wants."

"And this is why you sit up all night, staring at the bathroom door?"

"If Queenie comes for me, I can get away before she tries to do the decent thing."

"Could this be all going on in your imagination?" Mike asked.

"It's a possibility," Mr Winters agreed. "But I've seen enough of the wet footprints her ghost leaves behind, so I don't think that's the case."

"Don't you think you'll be more comfortable if you go to bed and let yourself get some proper sleep?"

"It sounds delightful," Mr Winters admitted. There was an edge of sarcasm in his voice as he added, "But I don't think it will be so pleasant if I end up being woken by Queenie's wrinkled wet fingers pressing against my throat."

"I'll stand guard," Mike said. "I'll take over your chair and I'll keep an eye on the bathroom door whilst you go to sleep."

Mr Winters regarded him suspiciously. "What do you get out of this?"

Mike rolled his eyes. "If you get a good night's sleep, I get the reassurance that one of my residents is well-rested."

Mr Winters hesitated for a moment, but it was obvious from the longing expression in his weary eyes that he yearned to spend a night asleep in a comfortable bed. "And you'll stay awake?" Mr Winters asked warily.

Mike didn't bother to offer a bland reassurance. "Get into bed and get some sleep," he said firmly. "You can get a proper night's rest and then, tomorrow, we can get you some professional help. I don't know if it's guilt, sleep-deprivation, or some other condition, but I'm fairly sure we can get this resolved so you're not spending your nights wide awake and glaring at a closed bathroom door.

Mr Winters, fully clothed, was climbing into the single bed behind the chair that Mike now occupied. He was about to put his head on the pillow when he said, "If you think I'm seeing Queenie because of guilt, or sleep-deprivation or some other condition, why are you watching the door for me?"

"I'm doing that for your peace of mind," Mike explained. "Now get some sleep and we'll talk more in the morning." He would have said more, but he realised Mr Winters was already snoring. Congratulating himself on a job well done, Mike settled himself into the chair and promised himself he wasn't going to fall asleep. However, that thought was still at the forefront of his thoughts when he gave a yawn and slumped into a doze in the chair. The last thing he remembered seeing before he fell asleep was the way the room's dim light glinted against the bathroom door handle, as though someone inside the en-suite was about to open the door and climb out.

This was how Mike spent his final night at the Golden Years Care Home.

He awoke the next morning to find Tanya Hide standing over him, demanding to know why he had been sleeping whilst on duty and asking him to explain why Mr Winters was dead. Because he had no explanation, he could only apologise as she told him his services were no longer required at the Golden Years Care Home. And it was only because he happened to catch Mr Winters' name in a news story next to the job ads he was scouring that Mike learnt what had happened to the old man. It seemed the coroner was puzzled by all the water in the old man's lungs. It was almost as though he had died from a drowning.

11

Queen Anne

By Angelique Jordonna

"Isn't she absolutely beautiful, Danielle?" Christina lets out a sigh as she stares at the house before her. Her eyes sparkle in the light of the sun and I find myself smiling right along with her, even though the house creeps me out. I haven't been able to put my finger on it, but there's something wrong with the place. I play along because I enjoy seeing my wife happy and I'm going to have to get used to it.

"You know, even as a kid, I was fascinated by this place. I had all these vivid dreams about being the one who built it." She takes in the view, admiring the graceful curves and panel insets of the home. The large porch and brackets draw her in even more. My smile grows larger as I watch her, amused by her child-like happiness and excitement about our new purchase.

"Well, now she belongs to us," I respond. I do admire how the black and white exterior pops with all the green foliage surrounding the home. "And for being a 130-year-old home, there's not much work to be done on her. Mostly minor cosmetic stuff. Should be easy enough for us to do ourselves. I'm glad someone decided to take care of it over the years. Most of these homes need so much more work. It's sad."

I watch as Christina gazes at the two turrets on both sides of our new abode. I can almost hear her heart skip a beat in her chest. I knew this was love at first sight for her. She has always wanted a Queen Anne house, this one to be exact, and now it's all hers.

Well, ours.

She walks up closer to the home and runs her finger along the wooden railing of the stairs that leads up to the massive wrap-around porch. Her fingers are gentle with the material, just like in the heat of the moment when she touches me.

"We will have her restored to her former glory in no time," my soft voice breaks the brief silence between us. I smile at Christina while pulling my shoulder-length brown hair back into a ponytail. "Before we move in, I want to sand those floors and stain them. So, we will be visiting the hardware store pretty quick."

"The floor is perfect, though. I wouldn't change a thing about it." Christina snaps at me. She turns her head and the glare in her eyes says she's not willing to change her mind.

"Christina Marie, we talked about this. I was willing to get you the house of your dreams as long as I could make some changes to suit me. You know this isn't my style of home. I would have loved a little modern home with a nice picket fence. Compromise, we agreed."

"Yes, Ms. Yeager. I know what we talked about. You don't have to remind me. I think she's perfect the way she is, though, just like you. Absolute perfection." She runs a finger along my jawline and gives me a wink.

"Sucking up isn't going to work right now, love."

"But you said yourself that not much work is needed." Christina leans herself into me and smiles really big. She always knows how to get her way and she's never afraid to use it against me. Just one smile, one little grin. What can I say? I'm easy.

"It's not a real change. The floors are old, it's just bringing them back to life with a little color. While we are at it, you can pick out some paint for those walls. That wallpaper has to come down."

"Not the wallpaper! You said comprise, I get to keep the wallpaper. That's part of the charm of this place. It's meant to be here."

'Eehhhh, you're lucky I love you. No one else could ever have their way with me like this." I lean over and place a kiss on her, my teeth nip at her bottom lip and I feel a shiver rush through me. I want to say it's because of the kiss, but I get a feeling that someone or something is watching us.

"You can keep the wallpaper wherever you want except for the bedroom and the library. Those are my rooms and I'm doing them the way I want, agree?"

Christina huffs at me, but finally agrees to my terms.

"Now, let's get inside and figure out what we need to pick up from the store," I say as we head up the stairs. "We can really start by putting up a nice white picket fence over there and run it around the rest of the yard. That cemetery on the left of us is a little creepy. It's the main issue I have with this place."

I stare past the line of weeping willows into the cemetery right next door. The things you do and accept for the person you love. A creepy house and an even creepier cemetery. Never in my life would I have let someone talk me into buying a house that had the dead as neighbors.

"I think it makes the house even better," Christina lets out a laugh. "The neighbors will be quiet at least; you hate noisy neighbors."

"Let's just get inside and decide what we are going to do so we can get our stuff moved in." I shiver and struggle to pull my eyes away from the cemetery. "I really don't want to spend more money on rent while paying a mortgage, if I don't have to." I turn the handle on the door. A creaking sound echoes off the walls as it slowly swings open.

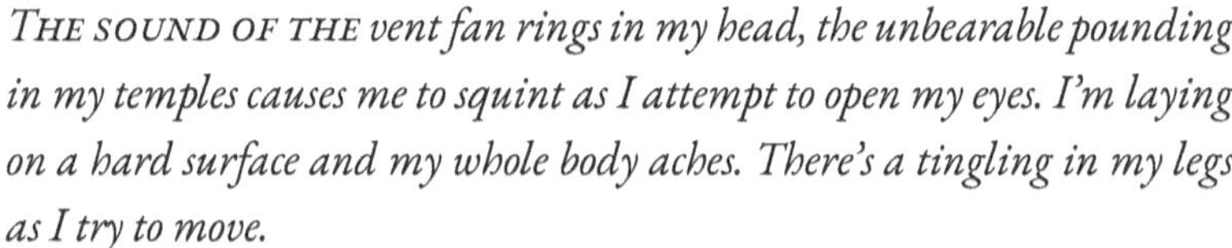

THE SOUND OF THE vent fan rings in my head, the unbearable pounding in my temples causes me to squint as I attempt to open my eyes. I'm laying on a hard surface and my whole body aches. There's a tingling in my legs as I try to move.

I slide my hand over the wooden finish of the floor and reach up to touch the tender spot on my temple. I wince from the touch. There's a dampness and I know it's blood from the blow I took before my world went black.

My head spins and I try to piece everything together, trying to figure out exactly where things started to change. What happened? How could I have prevented this? Everything in my brain is bleeding together as I do my best to calculate the last few weeks. Those last few weeks of hell. Torment. It's been pure agony.

The first week I know for sure was fine. Everything had been going smoothly. We stained the floors like I wanted to. We fixed knobs, replaced hinges, moved our belongings in. We laughed and enjoyed our time together. We danced slowly in front of the fireplace, and we made love in various rooms of the house. It was perfection. I, being in love with her and her being in love with the house. This damn house. It corrupted her from the inside out. It took her quickly. I'm afraid she may be lost to this gruesome structure for good.

I squeeze my eyes shut tightly when I hear something behind me. A breath sweeps across the back of my neck, and I do my best to not let out a sound. Not a single peep. I grind my teeth together and hope whatever it is will go away. Goose bumps form on my skin when its hair touches my cheek. Sweeping across my flesh as it settles on top of me.

The weight of this thing on me steals my breath away and a light touch of fingertips runs down my shoulder to my exposed breast. Her breath comes out in ragged bursts, and I can almost see my Christina before me. Those dark tight curls hang loosely in front of her face. I reach out to move them to the side and it's there. Her face contorts, a smile spreads, revealing menacing jagged teeth that appear to shine in the darkness.

She snaps her jaws open and closed several times, the grotesque figure leaving drops of drool on my face. I want to scream out, but it would be pointless because no one would hear me. Her nails dig into my flesh, piercing the skin of my biceps as she holds me to the ground, and I feel her grind her hips against me.

"Join me," words come from her mouth, but the voice is not hers. It's raspy and seems to be coming from the pits of hell.

"Give her back to me and we will just leave," I beg the beast inside of her. My voice feels strained, and I realize her hands are around my throat, fingers tightening their grip.

"No one escapes this place. No one escapes the Queen." My ears catch a faint laughter in the background, and I feel like I'm surrounded by pure evil. I can't breathe. My hands grasp at hers, trying to pull them away from my neck. There's no escape for me, though. My mouth opens and a scream finally erupts from my throat.

———◆O◆———

"WAKE UP, DANIELLE. WAKE the fuck up." Christina is shaking me, and I'm drenched in sweat. A little light shines through and my eyes begin to adjust to the dim room. Christina is beside me and her face is consumed with concern.

"That must have been some dream. You were gasping for air and then you started screaming. You scared the shit out of me."

"I..." I try to speak, my hands rub at my neck, trying to release it from the burning sensation left from her hands wrapped tightly around it. I look into her eyes to make sure she's really there.

"Are you alright?" Christina wraps herself around me and holds on tightly. I melt into her warmth, glad to be back from that horrible world I was momentarily trapped in.

"You weren't you. Something had..." I think about my words for a moment. "Something was living inside you. It turned you into some kind of beast. Your teeth, they were so sharp. It was horrible. You were trying to kill me."

"That's absurd, Danielle. Look at me, no sharp teeth. I would never hurt you."

"I know you would never hurt me, Christina. You weren't you, though. You were someone else. Something else. It was like you were possessed by something."

"No more horror movies for you, not for a while at least." Christine lets out a giggle, and it takes me back to the dream. The laughter in the background as she was trying to strangle me. I shiver and she pulls me closer to her.

"Go back to sleep. I've got you," she whispers softly in my ear.

I shut my eyes, but sleep does not come quickly. I don't know if I'll ever sleep again. Especially with dreams like that. Never in my life have I had a nightmare and I do not plan on letting it happen again.

Her breath hits the back of my neck and I shiver again. "It was just a dream," I tell myself. I repeat it over and over in my head until I feel comfortable enough to let myself drift off.

I WAKE TO THE sound of the piano and the smell of breakfast being cooked. I blink my eyes several times to get the blurriness to go away while stretching my limbs. My throat still burns.

"Breakfast is almost done," Christina yells up the stairs at me. "Better get yourself moving, lazy girl!"

I find myself stretching again as I try to get the rest of my body moving. It takes a few moments, but my feet finally hit the floor and I make my way down toward the kitchen. The piano music gets louder as I pass the closet door beneath the stairs and then fades a little as I walk into the kitchen.

"Do you hear that?" I whisper. "It sounds like someone playing a piano. I thought you had the radio on."

Christina turns her head to the side and listens. I can tell she's straining to hear anything. "Hhmmm. I don't hear it. Just the popping of the grease and the hum of the fan."

"I feel like I'm losing it. I swear, there's piano music. It was louder by the closet door." I walk back towards the stairs and find myself at the door. The music grows louder. The notes sound mournful, the sadness bleeding through with every single note that's being played.

"Come here. You are telling me you don't hear that?"

Christina stands next to me and shrugs her shoulders. "Don't hear a thing. Maybe you're just stressed and need something to take your mind off of everything. I can do that for you." She tugs at my shirt, trying to pull it over my head.

"Seriously, I'm going crazy and all you can think about is sex." I lean closer, putting my ear to the wooden door. My hand touches the handle and I pause, fear rising up in my belly. If I don't open the door, if I just walk away, would it finally stop?

Christine puts her hand on top of mine and twists the knob for me. I step back and let the door swing open. A blast of cold air hits us and she shakes from the draft. The music gets louder.

"Ok, I can hear it now. That's really odd."

"So, I'm not nuts?" I ask her.

She walks into the closet and pulls the string in the middle, filling the little room with light. The music stops.

"Yep, that's not weird at all," she says as she places her hand on the wall, feeling around. She slowly works her way around the room.

"What are you doing?" I ask as she starts touching the last wall.

"I knew it, I fucking knew it," she half screams as she pushes in on a section of the wall and it begins to move. "I always heard stories about a secret room! This is so exciting." She looks at me, her eyes gleaming with joy.

"Ya, like totally exciting. Weird music coming from inside the walls. A secret doorway. Not creepy at all."

"Maybe it's a music box or something. Let's look. Go grab a flashlight."

"I'm not going in there. Not going to do it. You're on your own here. I'm ready to pack and move." I turn to leave, and she grabs my hand.

"Please, get a flashlight. Don't make me go look on my own." She bats her eyes at me, and I see a sadness in them and it starts to play with me.

"Damn it, I hate you sometimes."

I walk away and am back minutes later with a flashlight in hand. "If there's a dead body in here, we are leaving and never coming back, I swear." I flip on the light and shine it into the darkness on the other side. Wooden stairs lead down into what looks like a basement. I take a deep breath in and slowly release it.

"Want me to go first?" Christina asks as she takes the flashlight from my hand and begins descending the stairs ahead of me. I try to talk myself out of following her, but I know I can't let her go by herself. There's no telling what is down there.

At the bottom of the steps, she finds a switch and flips it up, lighting up the whole room. The stone walls and concrete floor make it look like a massive dungeon. The décor draws me in, though. An old, red, Victorian couch sits against one wall. A table and side chairs to match.

In the middle of the room, a beautiful grand piano sits on a large ornate rug. Reds and golds run through the material, making intricate patterns that catch my eye.

"Wow, this is beautiful," Christina gasps as she steps around the piano and wipes some dust off of the bench. She takes a seat and runs her fingers over the ivory keys. "It sounds like it's still in tune."

"Maybe we should go back upstairs. I agree it's beautiful, but it shouldn't be playing itself."

Without thinking, I run my fingers along the smooth surface of the piano, drawn to the instrument before me. Remembering the days of my youth when my parents forced me to take piano lessons. Those days, I would rather have been outside playing with my friends.

"We should have a party. Invite people over to hang out down here. It's a perfect spot for a little get-together, don't you think?"

"I think, maybe, you're crazier than I am. Let's go back upstairs." I say once again. "Maybe we should get the blueprints and the history of this house so we can know what we are dealing with."

"You're no fun." Christina pouts as she stands up and follows me back upstairs. "And there's nothing wrong with this house. It's been around since I was a kid. A sweet old couple lived her for many years, and I believe the house has been in their family since it was built in the 1890s."

"So why is it not in the family anymore? Why did they finally sell it off?"

"I don't know. Perhaps there was no one else to hand it down to. Sometimes family lines die out. It happens. And now, it's ours."

"You aren't a little curious about any of it? I'm going to head into the library after I eat and see what the internet has to say about this place. Should have done it before we bought it, but you were so excited…"

"Well, you enjoy your search. I am going to go back downstairs and see what else I can find. We will do research in our own ways."

"I'll say it again. You're crazier than I am." I pour myself a cup of coffee and sit down at the counter, waiting for a plate of food to come my way. I watch as the beautiful woman before me smiles to herself. Happy about the new find. She slides a plate of food in front of me and gives me a wink.

"You always try to find the worst in things. Just enjoy having a beautiful home where we can finally start a family. Some kids and a dog. Growing old together, sitting on the porch on nice days."

"I'll enjoy the home after I know it's full history. It doesn't hurt to know details about things. Plus, maybe it will make me feel comfortable here. Right now, it still gives me the creeps. And with the nightmares I've been having ever since we moved in, it doesn't help."

"Like I said, enjoy your search and I will enjoy mine." She finishes her glass of juice and stands. "I'm going back downstairs to see if there's any other cool items. Give me a kiss and go do your research."

I lean in and whisper to her, "You're lucky I love you."

She giggles and walks out of the kitchen. I can hear the stairs creak as she descends into the belly of the house. The hairs on my arms stand on end as I feel fingertips trail down my back, and I know I am not alone.

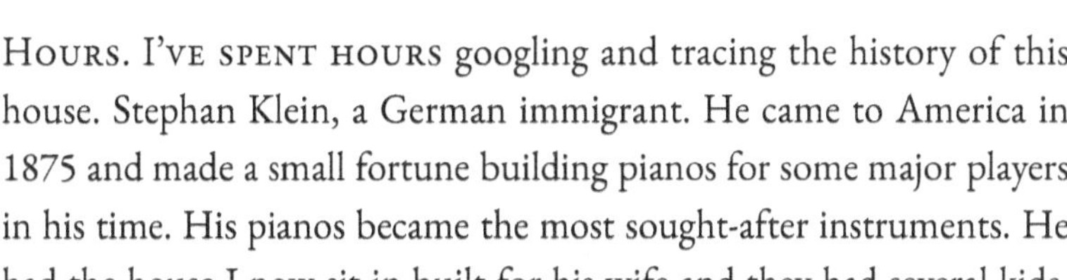

HOURS. I'VE SPENT HOURS googling and tracing the history of this house. Stephan Klein, a German immigrant. He came to America in 1875 and made a small fortune building pianos for some major players in his time. His pianos became the most sought-after instruments. He had the house I now sit in built for his wife and they had several kids. His wife disappeared on June 16th.

Klein said she ran away with another man, but a few suspected he killed her for cheating. Lots of rumors, but no proof of anything. Stephan passed away in his late sixties and was buried in the cemetery next door, two of his kids were buried there before he joined them.

A son took over the property and continued building Klein Branded pianos, though their quality is said to have declined with the passing of the old man. Nothing is like an original, that's for sure. His wife disappeared as well. The house continued to pass down until the last Klein died off last year. The house sat vacant until lucky us bought it.

So, I've basically found nothing. The original owner, some small details of disappearances and deaths that were said to be natural causes.

So how does one disappear into thin air? No trace. Just gone. My mind runs away with some thoughts and ideas about what could have happened. Murders? Ghosts exacting revenge on those who lived there? Did they just want something different, so they moved away without a word?

And he graveyard next door is the family burial ground, the ones they found were all laid to rest there. But where did the few lost ones go? I'm sure they are buried somewhere in the house. No one can tell me differently. I can feel it in my bones. Being a wife in this family was a death sentence.

I hear the piano start up and listen as a classical piece serenades me. I had no idea Christina could play like that. I didn't even know she was musically inclined at all. I stand and twist my body, trying to get my back to crack. When the motion fails, I make my way to the steps, listening to each one creak beneath my weight as I make my way downstairs.

Christina is sitting behind the piano, her eyes closed. I walk up behind her and watch as her fingers dance across the keys. She seems so comfortable. I'm amazed by her. I place my hand on her shoulder, and she jumps.

"Oh my God! You fucking scared me. You need to let someone know when you're coming." She twists on the bench and turns to face me.

"I had no idea you even knew how to play a piano. That was beautiful." I sit on her lap and lean in to kiss her. Her lips are soft pressed against mine and I feel something stir inside of me.

"I've never played piano before in my life, babe. You know that. I just looked at the music and, well..." she goes quiet for a few moments. "It just made sense to me. I don't know how."

"So, like an idiot savant?" I laugh as I say the words.

"Well, more idiot than savant," she smiles at me as she says the words. "Did you find anything in your research?"

"Nope. Learned about some of the owners. Family cemetery next door. A few wives who disappeared over the years. Nothing too detailed, though. The man who had the house built, though, was a piano maker. And I see his name on this piece. If he made it and not his son, it could be worth a lot of money. We should have it appraised."

"Appraised, for what? We are not going to sell it."

"It could pay for the whole house, though. We would have no mortgage if it's an original."

"It's mine, and it's not going anywhere," Christina snaps at me. She attempts to stand up and I almost fall from her lap.

"Ok, we can keep it. Still would be nice to know who built it."

"It was built by the one and only Klein. It says so right here in this engraving." She traces her fingers over the name on the front panel of the piano and I see her smile. Her teeth seem to shine brighter than before, and I swear I almost see a sharpness forming on them. "Oh, guess what I found while looking around down here?"

I'm quiet, not saying anything. There's no telling what is hidden in this dungeon. Finally, with as much humor as I can muster up, I say, "It wouldn't be a dead body, would it?"

"Hush, that's not funny. I found some diaries hidden behind a loose stone over there. They look really old."

Christina hands me two leather-bound books. A smell of mildew and death intrudes my nostrils and I almost gag. "These smell horrible," I say as I toss them back at her.

"You're being a bit dramatic." She places the items close to her nose and takes in a long, deep breath. "Really, I don't smell anything. They are pretty well preserved. Your senses are all jacked up. Are you sick or something?"

I think to myself, which one if us is really the sick one? I heard the piano when she could not. I can smell the death on those books, and she can not. I feel the wretched presence of something in the house, and she is oblivious to it.

"How about I read these over the next few days, and I can give you a rundown of what they say? Then you don't have to worry about whatever it is you're smelling." She holds the diaries close to her and starts moving toward the stairs. "You can take me to dinner tonight and afterward we can lie in bed, and I will read to you.

Being in bed with that scent doesn't sound like a fun night, but I don't want to argue with her at the moment. I just nod my head in agreement and follow behind her.

"Do you mind if I try to take a nap before going to dinner? You know I didn't sleep well last night."

"Sounds like a plan, Danielle. I'll start reading this and I'll wake you in a bit." Christina wanders into the living room and plops down on the couch. Her fingers stroke the leather material of the books before she unties the string wrapped around them and slowly opens a book. I watch her for a few moments, wondering why she is so fascinated with everything about this place. She glances up at me for a moment and gives me a grin. I smile back and then make my way upstairs to our room, lying down on the soft bed and attempting to drift off.

⚬

I WATCH AS SHE is slowly withering away. It started with her spending a few hours a day at the piano, playing. I would talk her into coming up to eat, to sleep a little. Then she began refusing to even leave the bench. I would take her food down.

Now she doesn't even stop playing to eat. What used to be smooth, white, ivory keys are now ragged, splintering and tearing open her fingers. They are stained red. She keeps playing, though.

Her cheeks are sunken in and her skin, once Carmel in tone, is pale white. I wipe tears from my eyes as I push away a few strands of hair on her face; she doesn't even glance at me, she just keeps playing. I back away from her as a smile takes hold of her face and I see those jagged teeth appear.

"You need to stop this. Just stop." I say, barely loud enough for even myself to hear.

"I can't. She won't let me." Is the reply I get. I see tears form in her eyes and she keeps playing.

I don't understand her words until I glance down at the floor near her feet. A pair of hands coming out of the floor are wrapped around her ankles, locking her in place. Claws are dug into her flesh, and she whimpers as they tighten and did in even more.

"She won't let me go," Christina cries out as her fingers keep a sullen melody going on the piano.

I rush to her and crawl beneath the piano. My hands work feverishly to get her loose. I pull at the clawed hand, smashing the long, slender fingers beneath mine. Nothing works.

"I'll be right back. I have to get something to get the hands loose."

"She's not going anywhere," the raspy voice comes from her lips, and I see her eyes darken. Her fingers move quicker across the keys, and she begins to

rock back and forth. The gleaming teeth snap at me as her head twists to the side.

I run up the wooden stairs and out to the garage. I rummage through boxes until I finally found a hand saw. I hold it up and take a gulp of air. My lungs hurt from not pacing myself and I struggle to breathe. I know I can't rest just yet, though.

I stumble while heading down the staircase and fall the rest of the way. The saw digs into my stomach and I feel the tiny teeth as I pull it from my skin. The cut is deep and I can see tissue poking out through the cut. It burns, but I force myself up and continue on my path to save her.

I drop to my knees and lay on my stomach, almost screaming out as the gash hits the floor beneath me. I work quickly, cutting close to the floor, trying to remove the hand from where it protrudes. Sprays of blood hit my face and sting my eyes as I continue the process. After what feels like hours of sawing, one hand comes free, and I begin to work on the other. Halfway through the process, I see fingers working their way up through the rug and they latch on to my Christina again.

I crawl backward at the sight. Defeated. She is lost to this house. To this piano. If I can't find a way to release her, she will surely die here.

I attempt to stand, leaning back into the cold stone wall. It's no longer a hard surface, and I feel myself being sucked into the mushy mass behind me. It's like being pulled into quicksand and I struggle to make my way out. A scream explodes from my mouth as I am sucked completely into the structure and surrounded by blackness.

⸻◆⸻

"DANIELLE, WHAT THE HELL! Wake up." My whole body is shaking, and I can feel my face covered in wetness. Tears? Blood? At this point, I don't know. I'm just happy to be back in bed with Christina beside me. "Your dreams have been out of control recently. What's going on?"

Christina leans herself into me and wipes some of the dampness from my cheeks.

"It was horrible." I cried. "You were being held in place, unable to move. All you could do was keep playing the piano. Like, these hands were coming out of the floor, and you couldn't get free. I tried to help. But... I couldn't save you. And the house was trying to kill me. And you still weren't you, even though sometimes you came through and would ask me for help."

"It was just a dream. I'm right here. I'm completely fine. I've just been reading while you slept. I should have woken you sooner." Christina smiles at me. No sharp, jagged teeth. No raspy voice. I try to find comfort in being close to her. Knowing everything was actually fine, but I can not.

"These diaries are interesting. Why don't we go downstairs, make some sandwiches and I can tell you about what I've found out so far?"

I shake my head, unable to find words at the moment, and I move to the edge of the bed to get up. My stomach burns. I place my feet on the floor and I pull my shirt up slightly. I find tiny little holes across the flesh, and they are bright red and irritated. I quickly pull the material down to cover the marks, hoping Christina wasn't paying attention.

⸺◆⸺

I SIT AND STARE at the sandwich before me. My fingers fidget with the tablecloth, and I'm completely silent. I can't get the images out of my head from the dream. It seemed so real. The images replay over and over in my head. Those long thin fingers with daggers for nails. The wall pulling me into it. Those sharp jagged teeth and a voice saying she could not be let go.

Over and over, the images would not go away.

"Hey, you need to eat something. It'll make you feel better." Christina breaks my silence and brings me back to this world. I pick up the sandwich and take a small bite as she continues to talk.

"So, these diaries were written in the very late 1890s. Sounds like Klein's wife was the one who wrote them. She started writing when he built the piano for her downstairs. She was so excited to have her own special model, one built just for her. But it sounds like things were not going well with him. And it sounds like he may have been abusive. She was scared of him. She would hide out downstairs and play piano to escape his anger. She thought he was just overworked and needed a break or something. I don't know, some of it was confusing and hard to read."

"I know in my research, it said she just disappeared. He said she ran away with another man because she was cheating on him."

"Actually, she was having an affair, but it wasn't with another man. She was in love with the maid of the house. They had a secret romance. It lasted for a few months until he finally found out and things between them became even worse. He locked her in the basement and wouldn't let her out. I have a feeling the maid disappeared as well."

"So, he locked away his wife and killed the maid? Where did she disappear to then? I mean, when he died, no one found another body here." I start to think about all the places on the property someone could hide a body.

"I don't know. Her diaries were hidden in the wall, so he must not have known about them, or he placed them there at some point. I think he killed her because her writing becomes erratic, and she starts to get delusional. Taking about the house being haunted, that it had possessed her husband, and he was going to kill her. He most likely did at some point."

"Now to figure out where he stashed her body."

"Wait, you said that in your dream, hands were coming up out of the floor beneath the piano. Perhaps he buried her under the floor in the basement. Placed the piano on top of it so no one would know. I'm going down there to look."

"You are really insane. I told you, if there's a body, we are moving. I don't care. I'm not doing dead people in my house."

"But hear me out! What if we solve a case that's well over a hundred years old? Wouldn't that be exciting?"

"I can't believe I married you sometimes," I respond to Christina. "We are completely opposite of each other."

"But you love my cuteness and sense of humor. You said so yourself." She gives me a little wink and begins to leave the room. She turns around when she reaches the doorway. "You coming with me? I may need help pushing the piano out of the way. I know it has wheels on it, but it's still pretty heavy."

I let out a sigh and take another bite of my sandwich. I don't like this at all, but I know if she's down there, we need to get her out of the house and have her buried in the cemetery. Everyone deserves a proper burial. "I guess I should grab the flashlight again, just in case."

"You're the bestest! Look at you thinking ahead." Christine lets out a little laugh and heads to the closet area. I sit for a moment, trying to talk myself out of this craziness, but I know this could be the answer to stopping all of those horrible dreams.

I grab a small flashlight from the junk drawer and begin that fateful walk into the basement. I have an overwhelming sense of dread running through my whole body as the old steps creak beneath me. The close I get to the bottom step, the worse the feelings get.

Christina is sitting in front of the piano, tinkering with the keys when I reach my destination. Her eyes are blank, and she sits. Her body begins to rock as she starts playing. The music is more upbeat than the other times I've heard her play. And then that smile. Twisted.

It takes me back into my dreams, and I tremble. My skin crawls as the music echoes off the walls. I am stuck with the decision of staying or walking away. Leaving her here in this house or trying to get her out. Could she be possessed like the original owner was said to be?

"Christina, are we going to do this, or are you going to just play that thing all night?"

She jumps a little when I speak, the smile leaving her face, and a darkness takes over. Her eyes go black and I take a step back, and then another.

"Where are you going?" She asks. "I need help moving this piano."

"I...the wheels seem to be in good condition. You should be able to push it without my help. I mean..."

She cuts me off. "I need your help, Danielle. With it sitting on this rug, it's a little harder to move. We can do anything together, though. You always say that." There's a sweetness in her voice, and a sadness takes over her eyes. "We have to make sure nothing is there. She deserves to be found if we can. That's a long time to go without anyone knowing where you are. It's heartbreaking. Please, help me."

She reaches her hand out to me. My mind has to be playing tricks on me. It's only her here. Nothing evil. It's only her. I reach my shaking hand out to her and she pulls me into her. Her soft breath flows across my neck, and her teeth nip at my ear.

"We can just go upstairs and enjoy each other." I whisper to her.

"How about we finish here, and I will treat you to something special later. Does that sound good?"

That smile, it's gets me all the time.

We begin to push the massive piano to the side. A wheel gets hung up on something and it becomes a struggle, but after several minutes we have it pushed to one side of the room and Christina begins to roll the rug up. Before she's halfway through, I see a wooden door built into the concrete floor.

"Who puts a door in a concrete floor?" I ask. "If I was going to bury a body, I would have dug the hole and filled it in with more concrete. Smoothed it over so no one could tell."

"But this way, he would still have access to her, right?"

It's disturbing how she connects things sometimes. It's also what makes her interesting. At times like this, however, I wished she would keep her insights to herself.

She grabs the handle of the door and tries to pull up. It moves slightly and then drops back down. She tries a few more times before stopping and giving me a look.

"This may be heavier than the piano," she says. I know this means she wants me to do it. Without making her ask, I take the handle and pull upwards. I get it up just enough to stick my knee under and use that to help me swing it all the way open.

I look down into the blackness of the hole, hoping that it's just an empty space, dreading finding an actual body in there. I turn on the light and shine it down, but it doesn't cut through the dark.

"You won't see anything standing there. You have to get down there and shine the light around to see anything. Hand me the light, I'll do it."

"I've got this, Christina. I don't want you to get hurt or anything. I'll look."

I kneel and kind of hang the upper part of my body in the hole, one hand gripping the floor and the other grasping the light. It hits a spot and I strain my eyes to see. Is that a jawbone? Teeth? I begin to panic and pull myself out when I feel my hand slip. Hands grab my legs and I'm thankful Christina is there to help me. A slight tug on my ankles and I know I will be fine.

Instead, those hands push, sending me into the hole, and a giggling sound comes from above. There's a loud bang and the door closes. Boney fingers grab at me, and I'm being held in place by the remains of this missing woman. Could this be the missing wife of Stephan Klein? Or perhaps it's the maid that went missing. The son's wife? More hands wrap themselves around my limbs and I know that it's all of them.

I fight, banging on the door above me. Screaming to be let out. Faint laughing is the only response I get.

OFFICER ROWLAND IS HEARTBROKEN for the woman in front of her. The lady wipes at her cheeks, trying to dry the moisture streaming down her face. It's always tough when a person comes up missing. Even tougher knowing that most missing persons in this area are never found. Rowland would not be telling her that, though.

"Do you know if maybe she just needed some time alone? Were you guys arguing or anything?" Officer Rowland asked. "Perhaps she just went to town for something."

"No, things were great with us. We just moved in a few months ago. We were talking about starting a family. I just got back from the store. She had no reason to go into town. The door was standing wide open when I got here. Oh God, I'm so scared." Christina's whole body shook as she bawled.

"Well, there's nothing I can do at this moment, ma'am. We have to give it 72 hours of her being missing before I can even make a report. I will keep my eyes open for her, though, and you keep an eye on her credit cards to see if there are any hits on them. Maybe track her phone."

"Her phone was left in the kitchen. Her wallet and car keys are still here. She's just gone. Disappeared into thin air. I don't know what I'm going to do." Christina sobs even harder and the officer gives her an awkward hug, trying to console her.

"Is anything missing? Anything out of place in the house? Does it look like a break-in?

"Everything is here. She's the only missing thing in the house."

"Give it the 72 hours. If you don't hear from her, you can come to the station and file a report then. We will find her. Don't worry." Office Rowland hands Christina a card with her name and the station number on it and leaves the sobbing woman alone.

Christina wipes away more tears and then straightens up. "I deserve an Oscar for this," she thinks. When she's sure the officer is gone, she makes her way down into the basement. She takes a seat on the bench, and she begins to play.

12

SHE REIGNS IN BLOOD

BY AJ MULLICAN

"Who the fuck is stupid enough to be scared of a legend called 'the Flower Queen'?" Broderick laughs and rips the notebook out of my hands, tossing it into the campfire.

"Hey!" I jump up from my camp chair to try to grab it, but Holly stops me.

"Gabby, what the hell? Don't reach into the fire."

"All my notes were in there." I pout and plop back down. "You're an asshole, Brod."

He shrugs and pokes the charred notebook with a stick. "You should be thanking me. I just saved you from the most boring horror death ever."

"For one thing, she's the Thorn Queen, not the Flower Queen. And for another, who says she was going to kill *me*?"

"It happens in all the horror movies: The annoying nerd who researched the evil thing is, like, the first to die. It's statistics."

Holly dumps her beer on Brod's head and drenches him. "Grow up, Brod. If Gabby wants to research local folklore, then let her. She's not hurting you with it."

He scowls as he wrings out his hair. "She's gonna bore me to death."

"No one's killing anyone because Mom would kill us *all* if that happened." Holly pulls out a bag of marshmallows and spears one with a metal skewer. "She made us promise to all come back alive, remember?

'No fratricide in the forest.' You know when she brings out the four-dollar words, she means business."

"That's as stupid as Gabby's Flower Queen." Brod snatches a marshmallow and skewers it. "Mom knows nothing's going to happen on a dumb camping trip."

I hate being the youngest. Brod has the benefit of being old enough to buy us alcohol for the trip, but not so old that he cares about rules like Holly. She's here to make sure Brod doesn't do something truly stupid, like lure me into the fire by throwing my only notes in it. They're only a year apart, but people must change a lot in a year, because Holly would never be that idiotic.

The camp-out was Holly's idea. She thought it would be a fun send-off for me before college, and I didn't have the heart to veto her. At four years apart, Holly always said she felt like we weren't close enough.

Not that it's Holly's fault or anything. She tries, but we just don't share any interests. She likes boys and music and going out clubbing. I like books and hot cocoa and local folklore.

Like the Thorn Queen.

Here in northwest Washington State, most of the local lore has indigenous roots. Native American lore, which is *fascinating* on its own, but that's not what draws me to the Thorn Queen story.

What draws me in is her gruesome tale, and the fact that, while no one can quite pinpoint where the legend started, almost every single person who's told her tale insists she's not an indigenous myth.

They say she's older than that.

Did the ancient Mongolians bring her tale over the Bering Strait before the continents split? Is her origin in the Russian Chukchi region, or has it traveled even farther than that?

She sure sounds like an old Russian myth. While she doesn't have any direct ties to Baba Yaga, her story bears some similarities on the brutality front. Specifically, cannibalism of young forest-goers. Not necessarily children like Baba Yaga, but young people who venture into the Thorn Queen's domain.

Her original name is lost to time, I guess. No one knows what the Thorn Queen was originally called, or at least no one alive that I've found to ask about her knows. Some say that her name doesn't matter, that she wouldn't answer to it if I knew it because no one has survived meeting her to call her by her name. She just devours anyone who crosses her path. Anyone who enters her ring.

I know, I know, the whole "fairy ring" story is older than dirt. But this isn't a fairy ring story, I promise. It's a ring of flowers for one thing, not mushrooms, and if I'm being perfectly honest, the fae have nothing on the Thorn Queen's cruelty.

Brod snaps his fingers in my face, and I jump back to reality.

"Dude, Gab, what are you doing? You just kind of zoned out there."

I answer him with a scowl, pulling my now-charred marshmallow out of the fire and burning my fingertips as I tug it off the skewer. I stick my fingers in my mouth, sucking on them to soothe the burns.

Brod laughs as he goes for the first aid kit Mom made us bring along. "I think we have some aloe or something in here."

Never one to play the wounded cub, I get up and stalk off to the nearby spring to wash my hands. I'm not giving Brod the satisfaction of seeing how badly I burned myself, and I certainly don't need first aid from a jerk like him.

To my supreme annoyance, Brod follows me.

"What are you doing?"

"Making sure the Flower Queen doesn't snatch you while you're out walking in the woods alone."

I roll my eyes. "If you'd been listening, you'd know she uses a ring of roses to trap her victims. Do you see any flower rings here? No. So I'm fine."

"How do plants trap someone, anyway?" He scratches his head. "I mean, I could just step over them, couldn't I? Or walk away from them? Not super scary, if you ask me. Now, a ring of thorns would be cool. Then I might be a bit concerned. I could seriously scratch myself on something like that. Death by a thousand cuts!" Brod pantomimes stabbing me with a knife. I roll my eyes and kneel at the spring, shoving my hands in the cool water.

I gasp as the spring runs over my burned fingertips, shocking yet soothing at the same time. While I soak my hands, something catches my attention out of the corner of my eye. Across the stream, on the far bank, is a small thicket of bushes.

Rosebushes.

Growing in a ring.

Sure, it's not a perfect circle, and the ring of bushes is broken in places, enough for a person to walk through, so I guess it could be seen as just another wild thicket—nothing too suspicious to the average observer. It's enough to give me an idea, though.

"Hey, Brod, you think we could stay at this campsite overnight? I know we were supposed to hike onward, but I love the scenery here."

He lifts one shoulder, and picks wax out of his ear with his pinky. "Sure. Why not?"

I don't think he even notices the flowers across the way.

He probably doesn't suspect a thing.

By the time we get back to camp, dusk has fallen on the woods. Brod has the decency to assist me in setting up our tent, but before I can put my plan into action, he's out cold in his sleeping bag, snoring away. I'll have to wait until morning.

I stay up talking with Holly most of the night, too excited to sleep. My eyes keep darting over to where Brod sleeps, hoping to catch him up for a pee break during the night. Unfortunately, though, he's as still as a rock until long after sunrise. By then, Holly and I have already gotten up and dressed and started cooking breakfast. My plan will have to wait a little longer.

Finally, Brod tromps off in search of firewood after breakfast, and I scurry to catch up with him.

"Wait! Brod, c'mon. Don't leave me behind."

"Why?" he calls back over his shoulder. "You scared the Flower Queen is gonna get you?"

If I had any doubts, he just cinched my resolve to show him a lesson. I grab his arm to slow him down. "For the last time, she's the *Thorn Queen*. It's different."

"Whatever." He brushes me off like I'm some kind of mosquito.

I ball my hands into fists at my sides. Finding a new burst of energy, I push past him, stomping through the underbrush and clear through the spring where I washed my hands last night. Straight towards the thicket.

I'll show him.

"Gab, wait up!" Leaves and branches crunch behind me as he rushes forward. "Mom will kill me if you get lost out here."

I stop a couple feet shy of the rosebushes and spin around. "What are you gonna do to me, Brod? Mom's not here to tell me what to do, and I'm an adult now. I sure as hell don't have to listen to you."

Brod has almost caught up to me. He reaches for me, striding forward in his soaked jeans. "Gab, please. You're gonna get yourself hurt running around like that."

I can't let him catch me. He'll rat me out to Mom for sure. I take a step back—

—and trip, landing flat on my ass inside the thicket.

My legs and arms flail as I scramble to get to my feet. Shit! I was trying to trick Brod into chasing me here; I didn't mean to actually go inside the ring ...

With my eyes squeezed shut in fear, I thrash and scream, and something strong grabs my arm. I can't break its grip, which gets stronger the more I fight. Finally, in a crazy act of desperation, I go limp, hoping that whatever has me will get bored and let go. It tugs at my arm, and I hear Brod's voice in the distance.

"Gab, are you okay? You fell pretty hard there. Did you hit your head?"

Wait ... Brod's voice isn't so distant. I risk opening my eyes just a hair and see him standing over me. His face is a mask of concern, in total contrast to his earlier ribbing.

"C'mon. Let me help you up."

Once I realize that its Brod's hand gripping me, not *hers*, I shake it off and scramble to my feet without his help. We're both inside the ring of roses, and there's ... nothing. No mysterious, deadly woman. No creeping vines or vicious thorns.

I don't know if I'm more relieved or disappointed.

"But I fell into the ring of roses ..."

Brod looks around us, scratching his head. "Huh. What do you know? It's an actual ring of roses." A light reaches his dimwitted eyes, and he laughs. "Dude! It's just like the old kids' song. 'Ring around the Rosie.' I wonder if it's a reference to this queen of yours. You think the people who started the legend ever heard it?"

I roll my eyes. "Brod, that song is from England during the Plague. How would ancient inhabitants of the Northwest U.S. have heard it?"

"TV?" he suggests with a shrug.

The sheer idiocy makes me groan, and I stalk away, back towards camp.

"For fuck's sake, Gab, would you wait for me?"

I come to a halt just before reaching the spring. When I turn back to glare at my brother, I see him still standing in the ring, a confused expression on his face.

"What are you doing? Let's just get the firewood we came to get and go back," I say.

Brod blinks. "I can't."

I stomp back up the hill with a huff. "Fuck, Brod, quit goofing off. Let's go!"

He looks down at his feet and blanches. I've never seen him so white. "Gab, sis ... Maybe you should run."

Great, he's trying to scare me. "I'm not buying it, Brod."

With a trembling hand, Brod points to his feet. "Run."

I finally give in and look ... and scream as I see both of his feet impaled by several foot-long thorns. Blood oozes from the wounds, and as I watch, the thorns grow longer and thicker. Another spike appears, piercing his shin from behind. Bone splinters loudly as more thorns break through, and his jeans audibly tear. Brod grits his teeth with a groan, and I see now that he wasn't trying to scare me; he was trying to be brave for me.

"Run!"

Torn between saving my brother and self-preservation, I latch onto Brod's arm and tug as hard as I can. I pull and pull, but I can't bring his arm back across the edge of the ring. It's as though an invisible barrier holds him there, keeping him from moving beyond the rosebushes. Tears spring to my eyes, and I sob as I yank harder at his arm. More thorns grow through him, expanding into full-on branches covered in his blood. They grow up his legs, creeping towards his torso, lancing through him at an alarming rate.

"C'mon, Brod! If we just get you free of these thorns, we can get out of here." My voice wavers, giving away my doubt.

I don't believe anything short of a weed whacker or chainsaw can cut him loose.

Brod opens his mouth to say something, but whatever it was, it's drowned in the blood that comes spilling out. I scream as I look down and see that the thorns have pierced his chest and abdomen.

Jumping back, I barely miss getting stabbed myself as the thorns continue their exponential growth. One thorn cuts my palm as I wrench my hand back out of the ring, letting Brod go.

I gape in horror, frozen in place, as the thorns stab through his heart. Brod's body jerks and twitches, and he gurgles as more blood seeps from his mouth. Finally, his eyes turn glassy, and his body stills, save for one final twitch when a thorn emerges from his right eye socket, carrying the speared eye out with it.

"Gab! Gabby! I heard you screaming." Holly's voice trails up the hill from behind me. I whirl around and move to block her from seeing Brod's body.

"Holly, go back! Don't come any closer."

Typical for my big sister, she ignores my plea. She runs up the hill and pushes me aside. "Gabby, why were you screaming? Why were you—*Oh, my God!*"

I try to stop her, but Holly's too fast. She rushes into the ring and pulls on one of Brod's limp arms. The thorns shoot out, ejecting from the branches that grow out of our brother's body. They fly out like darts, dozens at once, leaving her looking like she ran headfirst into a cactus. A large, violent cactus. Holly screams as the thorns bury themselves several inches deep inside her body, but it's cut off by a thorn to the throat.

She drops like a rock, and suddenly I'm all alone.

As I stare at their dead bodies, the wind picks up, lifting my hair off my shoulders. A soft voice echoes with laughter, and a pair of feet enter my vision, coming to rest next to Holly's still-twitching form. The feet are bare, covered in dirt. As my eyes trail up, more details come into view. A flowing, tattered brown dress. Slender body. Arms wrapped in thorny vines. And finally, a woman's face, crowned in roses, with eerie white irises in her eyes, which cry bloody tears.

"Thank you," the woman says, her voice reverberating in my head. *"I was ever so hungry ..."*

My feet move of their own accord, pounding against the dirt to move me away from the gruesome scene. I tear through the stream, between the trees, across the forest to our campsite. Once I'm finally free of the nightmare, I stop and put my hands on my knees, bent over, gasping for breath.

When Holly says my name, I jump so hard I wonder if I've left my skin behind.

"Gabby! Where have you been? Brod got back ages ago with the firewood. He says you disappeared on him."

I blink, confused, as Holly and Brod appear from inside the tent. They seem perfectly fine, no thorns, no blood.

They're all in one piece.

Surging forward, I catch them both in a breathless hug. Brod and Holly gape at each other, their faces masks of confusion.

"Gab, what's going on? Why are you so affectionate all of a sudden?" Holly takes my hand in hers. "And what happened to your hand? Jesus, Brod, get the first aid kit. She's bleeding all over the place!"

Holly guides me to a camp chair, holding my hand, while Brod trots off to get the kit. I sit down, but my body shakes so hard I worry the chair will come apart. Watching Holly clean and wrap my hand, I keep seeing flashes of the thorn-speared Holly overlaid atop her living face. The images flicker in and out like an old movie reel, strobing violently. The effect makes me a little queasy, and I waver in my seat. Brod places a steadying hand on my shoulder. When I turn to him, his face has the same eerie, flickering appearance. It's like the ghost of Brod from a few minutes ago is haunting Brod right now.

"Relax, Gab. It's not as bad as it looks. Now that she's got the blood cleaned off, you can see it's not really that deep."

"You're alive ..." My voice is barely a whisper. "You're both alive ..."

My siblings exchange glances. "Huh?"

I shake my head to clear it before I inspect Holly's bandaging job. My hand throbs, but no more blood seeps out. Testing my fingers, I find them all mobile. However deep the cut may be, it appears I didn't sever anything important.

The pain in my hand is real enough. I definitely really cut it, but what happened in the thicket? How did Brod and Holly get back here, and where are all the thorns?

"Gabby, what happened? Where did you run off to?"

Ghost Holly superimposes itself over living Holly, blood spurting from the thorn wound in her throat as she talks. I gag and look away.

"Didn't Brod see it? The thicket?"

Brod frowns. "I didn't see any thicket, Gab. I was collecting firewood. I looked away from you for a nanosecond, and you were gone. We've been searching for you for an hour. We just came back to camp to see if you'd show up back here." He chuckles. "We were seconds away from calling the rangers to help us search for you."

An hour? The whole gruesome ordeal lasted just a couple of minutes. How can I have been gone for an hour?

"Well, at least you're safe now. We'll worry about where you went some other time; let's break camp. If we hurry, we can get back to the car before nightfall." Holly walks back to the tent and starts breaking it down, untying rope and pulling stakes. "This camping trip is officially over. That hand might need stitches."

"Stay ..." A ghostly voice echoes in the wind.

"Did you guys hear that?" I ask.

Brod looks up from helping Holly, and my eyes cross as I take in the horrific overlay of his dead body, the severed nerve of his speared eye wiggling as he moves. "What?"

"That voice ..." I stand up and get hit with a wave of dizziness. Plopping back down in the chair, I put my good hand to my head. "Oh, God!"

"What's wrong?" Holly asks.

I shake my head again, trying to clear it. "I'm just super dizzy all of a sudden."

The two Hollys frown. "Stay in the seat; don't try to stand up. I bet the sight of all that blood has you in shock or something."

She has no idea.

"Brod, get your phone out and find the nearest hospital. I think we should take Gabby there before we try to go home."

Ghost Brod flashes an evil grin as normal Brod follows Holly's order. I scoot forward in my seat, squinting at the screen to see what he's doing.

Brod isn't searching for hospitals.

Brod is searching for graveyards.

"Found one!" he exclaims as he presses a button to save the directions to his maps app. "If we hurry, we might get Gab there before she passes out from melodrama."

"I-I really think I'm okay," I say, cradling my bandaged hand to my chest. "I don't need a doctor or anything."

Holly rolls her eyes, and the phantom overlay grins evilly. "Don't be silly. Besides, if we brought you home with that hand like that and we didn't have a doctor look at it, Mom would murder us." The image of dead Holly makes a slashing motion across her hemorrhaging throat.

"We outvote you, Gab. Two to one. You'll never win this argument."

Brod's ghost twin winks his bad eye, the lids not quite closing because the thick thorn is still in the way.

I clutch my stomach and gag. "I think I'm gonna be sick."

While the two of them pack up the tent, I slowly get up and inch away from the campsite. Something's not quite right, and I don't understand how they can be simultaneously perfectly fine and torn to pieces.

The two Hollys look up, and the thorn-riddled Holly scowls. "Fuck, Gabby, get back here!"

I dart between the trees and break into a run, hoping the thorns in ghost Brod's body slow him down enough to keep him from catching me. When I hear footsteps tearing through the brush behind me, though, I know that's not the case.

He's after me.

Once again, I find myself at the stream, just a few yards from the thicket. I look left and right, hoping to see an avenue for escape, but the stream is at its most shallow here, and if I try to wade further down- or upstream, I'll just get swept away. It goes against my every instinct, but I have to run onwards.

I have to run for the thicket.

My only chance, my only hope is that I can reach the thicket in time, before Brod catches me.

I pump my feet, panting with the effort of running. A quick glance over my shoulder shows the dead Brod grinning insanely as my living brother starts to gain on me. I burst through a gap in the thicket and run smack into the woman from before.

"Yesssss," she hisses, her cold white eyes glinting with malicious glee, *"bring me food…"*

I open my mouth to scream, to warn Brod not to come after me, but she clamps a hand over it. I wriggle and kick, but it's no use. Her grip is stronger than iron. She turns me around, forcing me to watch as Brod gets closer and closer.

"Watch, little one ... Watch as your brother meets his fate ..."

A wall of thorns grows right in front of my eyes, and somehow Brod doesn't seem to see it. He keeps barreling onward, straight for it.

He runs headfirst into the thorns, and his eyes bulge as they pierce his body.

Once again, I'm left helpless as I watch my brother ripped to shreds by the plants. Once again, I listen as he gurgles and chokes on his own blood.

The woman laughs while Brod's body jerks in the final death throes. *"So delicious ... Now bring the sister ..."*

Tears stream from my eyes, and I try to bite the hand that holds me. It's no use, though; despite her ability to hold me in place, my teeth clamp together as though biting down on air. The woman cackles again, and she strokes my cheek with her other hand.

"Bring the sister, and you live ..."

I can't just give Holly over to this madwoman, but it's not like I'm super keen on dying right now, either. What can I do?

"Brod! Gabby!"

Oh, no ...

It's too late.

She's coming.

No matter how hard I struggle, I can't break the Thorn Queen's grip. She holds me in place, laughing mercilessly as Holly sprints up the hill. I watch in slow motion as it all happens again.

Once again, the thorns shoot out of the rosebushes, spearing Holly like so many darts. Once again, she gags on a thorn in her throat.

Holly falls to her knees, landing inside the rose ring. The Thorn Queen cackles, and she finally lets me go. I scramble over to Holly, cradling her head in my lap. I can't stop sobbing, can't stop the tears that stream from my eyes.

"C'mon, Holly," I say, hiccupping. "C'mon. Get up."

Her eyes blink slowly as she gasps for air. Red bubbles ooze out of the throat wound, and a fine mist of blood sprays with each exhale. Her body jerks and spasms, but within seconds she's still.

They're dead again. I just got them back, and they're already dead again.

The Thorn Queen bends and brushes tears from my cheek. I shrink away from her touch.

"You can save them, you know."

"How?" I sob. "You've killed them twice now."

She smiles, baring bloodstained teeth. *"Take their place ... Take their place and stay with me. Be my meal."*

I stroke Holly's hair as I hold her to me. "How do I know you'll honor your word?"

"I am older than lies. Older than treachery. I am from a time when the truth was all that existed, when fantasy and fable were not yet conceived."

I can save them ... if I die instead.

Something needles at the back of my mind, some inconsistency with the Thorn Queen's offer. I glance up at her with narrowed eyes. "Why are you willing to give up two victims in exchange for me? It doesn't make sense."

Again, she laughs, and she holds out a bloody-tipped thorn. *"You taste divine. Much sweeter than they do. Disbelief tastes so bitter, almost rancid."* She licks the tip of the thorn, and her white eyes roll back in her head. *"You believe. You acknowledge. Your blood will sate me for much longer than theirs."*

I believe ... Does she mean the legend? Am I tastier to her because I researched the legend?

"So, if I stay here, if I let you—*ahem*—eat me, they'll live?"

Her bloody grin reappears. *"They will not die by my hand, no."*

I suspect that's the closest I'll get to a straight answer. "What do I have to do? I'm already here, in your ring. You've got me now, so what else do I have to do to get you to leave them alone?"

"The promise of blood is all I need ..."

Her ghostly-white hand still holds the thorn out to me. I let Holly's body fall to the ground as I stand to take it from the Thorn Queen. As soon as my fingertips touch the slender spike, Holly's dead body fades away to nothing, leaving no trace. Brod's body follows suit, and in the blink of an eye, I see them off in the distance, alive and well and searching for me.

"Promise, and they live ..."

Realizing that there's a time limit on the Thorn Queen's offer, I grip the thick end of the thorn with my bandaged hand and hold it over my heart. I don't know how I could possibly pierce through bone and cartilage with it to reach the beating organ, but considering her thorns sliced clean through Brod's entire body, I suspect there's some magical property to them that makes them stronger than average rose thorns. I pause, inhale a deep breath, and jam the thorn into my chest.

I don't know what I expected to feel. Pain, of course. Sharp, stabbing pain.

What I didn't expect was euphoria.

My eyes roll back in my head, and I let out a sigh. Who knew dying could feel so *good*?

"Yessss ... Your blood is so delicious ..." The Thorn Queen wraps her hand around mine, around the thorn, and pushes it further in. I gasp and twitch, watching as her fingers merge with the thorn and spiky branches grow from her body. Unlike the thorns that grew through Brod, these thorns emerge from her skin like stiff, thick hairs, like parts of her that are simply getting longer and denser. Her nails also transform into thorns, and she strokes my cheek with them, slicing thick trenches in my skin.

"You're so succulent. So ripe." Rivers of blood run down my face and neck as she caresses me. *"You'll make a fine meal."*

"Gabby? Gabby, where are you?" I hear Holly's voice in the distance. She's within sight of the thicket, but when her eyes turn my direction, they glaze over. The rosebushes creak and groan as they grow thicker, blocking her from my view.

"They won't see you, pet," the Thorn Queen assures. *"No one will ever see you now."*

Her thorns continue to lance through me, each one sparking a fresh wave of ecstasy. I moan and shudder.

"Welcome to my thicket, pet." She places a soft, tender kiss on my torn lips. *"Now be a good girl and die for me ..."*

"Brod, what if we can't find her?" Holly sobs and shakes, and I put an arm around her shoulders to try to comfort her.

"She'll turn up, Hol. She's probably just playing some weird trick on us. You know, that whole Flower Queen bullshit. She's off hiding somewhere, and when the rangers find her, she's gonna feel really stupid for putting them through all that trouble."

I'm not sure if Holly believes me, but it's all I have. We searched for hours for Gabby, well into the night, and now the rangers are combing the whole forest for her.

The weird thing about it is the blood they found. Pools and pools of it, up by a thicket of rosebushes. Enough for three or four people, they said, and fresh. That sparked a whole new line of questioning from the rangers, but since Holly and I didn't have a drop of blood anywhere on us, they finally let us go to continue the search.

"Cops are on the way, Hol. They'll find her. Don't worry."

Sirens echo in the forest, and the police lights flash through the trees. We wait at the edge of the parking area for them. Mom and Dad showed up shortly after the rangers, after we realized we really couldn't find

Gabby on our own. Mom's sobbing as hard as Holly, and like me, Dad's trying to comfort her.

I don't think we'll ever comfort them.

I don't think we'll find Gabby.

"Holly," I say, keeping my voice low as the police pull to a stop, "do you remember?"

"Remember what?" she says through her sniffling.

"Dying."

Holly pushes me away. "You're fucking sick, Brod!" She stomps off to where Mom and Dad stand talking to the cops. I stay off to myself, rubbing my eye, which for some reason is sore and achy.

No, more than sore. More than achy.

It feels more like a stabbing pain. Like a thorn jabbing in my skull.

It's sad that Holly doesn't remember. I do. I remember my death—two times over—and somehow, I just know that Gabby did something to bring us back.

There might be something to her Thorn Queen myth, after all ...